Pocket Scientist

CHEMISTRY EXPERIMENTS

Mary Johnson

Illustrated by Colin King

Editor: Helen Davies

Contents

First published in 1981 by
Usborne Publishing Ltd,
Usborne House, 83-85 Saffron Hill,
London EC1N 8RT, England.

Printed in Great Britain

About this book

This book is full of safe and simple experiments using equipment and chemicals that you can find at home. There are experiments to do to make a gas, split water and copperplate a key, and you can test fizzy drinks to see what makes them fizz. There are tests to do, too, on sweets and washing powders and you can make bath salts and invisible inks and find out how they work.

Over the page there are some hints on being a chemist, and a list of useful things to collect for your "lab". On pages 62-63, there are lists of all the equipment you need for each experiment.

Before you do any experiments read through the guidelines and safety hints on pages 6-9. If you follow these carefully, your experiments will be more successful.

Being a chemist

Everything around us is made up of chemicals. Chemistry is the study of chemicals and how they behave when you mix them and heat them, cool them or do other things to them. The ways the chemicals behave are called chemical reactions. Chemical reactions are happening all the time. For instance, when food is cooked, when a bicycle goes rusty and when coal burns, chemical reactions are taking place.

Chemists do experiments to study the way chemicals react and find out more about them. Often they can work out what will happen before they do an experiment because they know the special characteristics, or "properties" of the different chemicals. They do experiments to check their theories.

Through their work they can create new substances, such as plastics and man-made fibres, and discover chemical reactions which are useful in medicine and industry.

This book shows you how to do simple experiments with chemicals such as lemon juice, washing soda and salt. From these experiments you can find out the properties of the chemicals and see how they react, just like a real chemist.

Setting up your lab

For your lab you need a place with a table or bench where you can do the experiments, and some shelves or a cupboard where you can keep your chemicals and equipment. It is useful to be near a sink, too. You should not do the experiments near food. Always put your chemicals away when you have finished, and keep them out of reach of young children.

Things to collect

Jam jars with lids
Bottles with tops
Sticky labels
A pen or pencil
Drinking straws
Roll of paper towels
An old, blunt knife
An old tablespoon
Plastic teaspoons
Ruler
Notepad
A cloth and an old toothbrush
  for cleaning equipment

OVERALL OR APRON TO PROTECT YOUR CLOTHES

NEWSPAPER TO COVER TABLE OR CARPET

Above is a list of the things you need in your lab. You can do most of the experiments in jars, but for a few, test-tubes are better. You can find out where to buy test-tubes, and other useful equipment, on page 61. There are some suggestions for equipment to make yourself on pages 56-59.

1 Chemicals

You will find most of the chemicals you need at home. Keep small amounts of them in labelled jars or bottles.

You can find out where to buy more unusual chemicals, and things you do not have at home, on page 60.

Doing experiments

On the next few pages there are some hints and guidelines to help make your experiments successful. The experiments may not always work first time, though, and chemists sometimes have to repeat experiments several times. If one of your experiments does not work, read the instructions again and try to work out what went wrong. Here are some important points to remember.

1 Read all the instructions for an experiment before you start, so you know what to do, and make sure you have everything you need.

2 Make sure all your equipment is clean and dry. If it is wet or dirty, the experiment may not work.

3 Measure the amounts of chemicals you use very carefully. You can find out how to do this over the page.

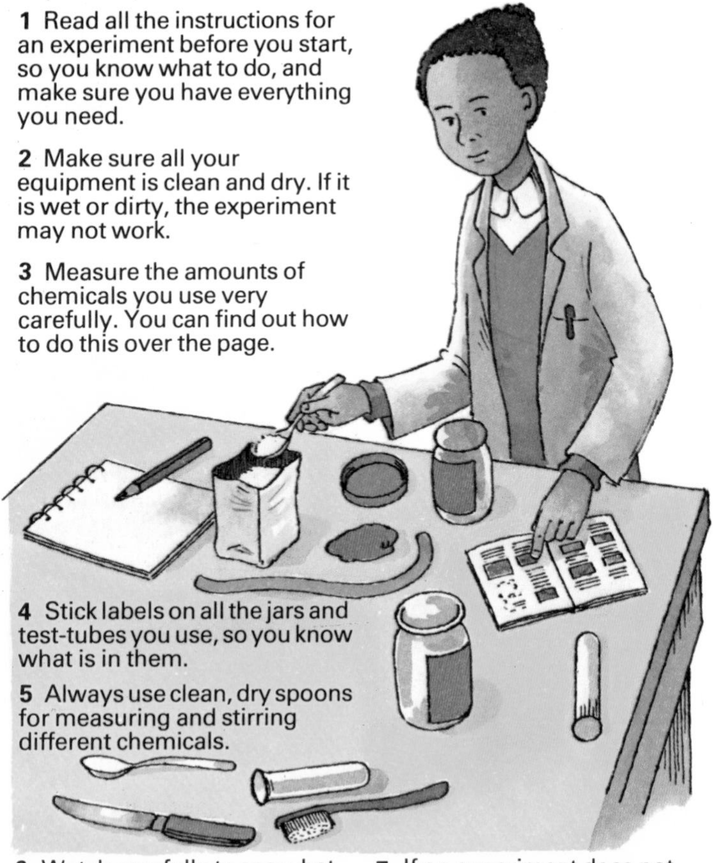

4 Stick labels on all the jars and test-tubes you use, so you know what is in them.

5 Always use clean, dry spoons for measuring and stirring different chemicals.

6 Watch carefully to see what happens in the experiment. Note down any changes in colour, bubbles of gas or other reactions.

7 If an experiment does not work, wash all the equipment and start again. If it keeps on going wrong, try using a completely different set of equipment.*

** There may be something on one of the jars or test-tubes which will not wash off.*

As soon as you finish an experiment,* wash all the equipment in warm, soapy water, rinse it well, and dry with a paper towel. If you do not wash your equipment straight away, it may be very difficult to get clean.

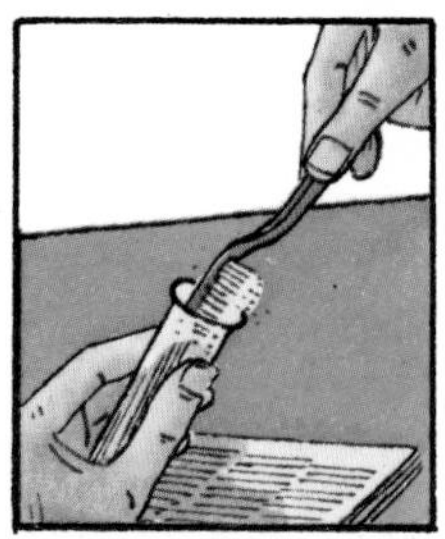

An old toothbrush is good for cleaning test-tubes and scrubbing ring-marks off jars.

You should always label the jars or test-tubes you use for the chemicals in an experiment, even if there are only two of them. It is very easy to forget which is which during the experiment.

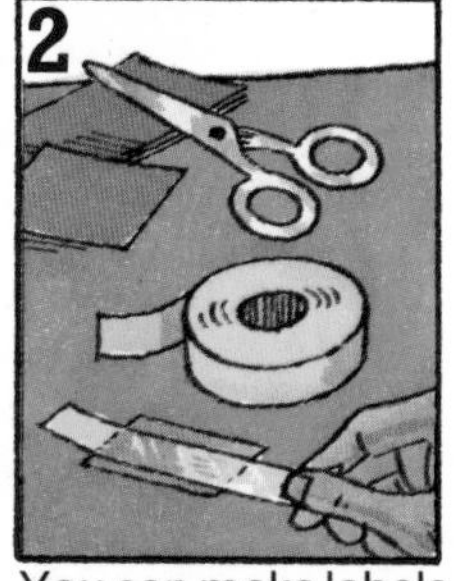

You can make labels from paper and sticky tape, or buy sticky labels from a stationery shop.

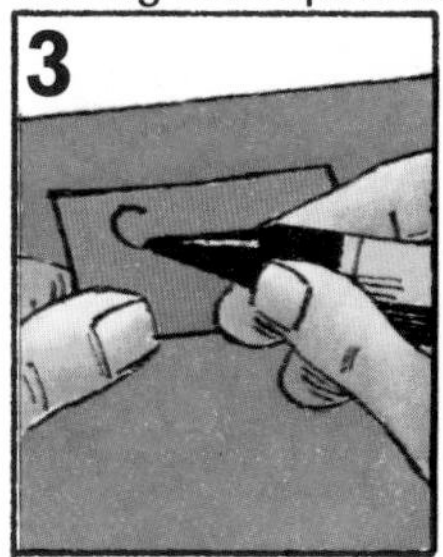

Write the labels in pencil or crayon so they do not smudge.

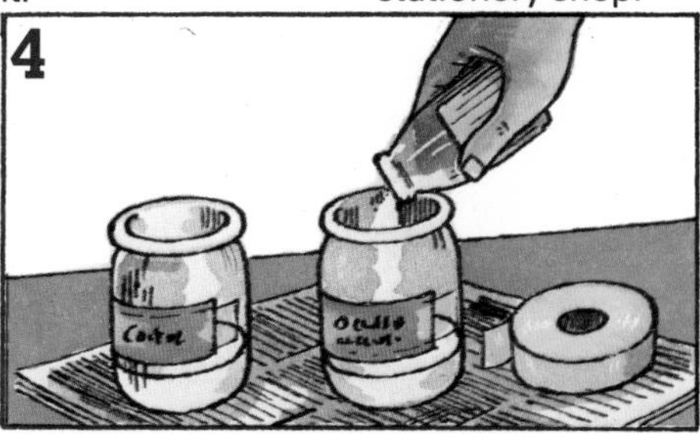

It is easier to write the labels before you stick them on the jars. To avoid spilling the chemicals, stick the labels on the jars before you put the chemicals in.

** Pour chemicals away down the sink or lavatory – see "Safety hints" on the next page.*

Measuring

It is very important to measure out chemicals carefully and accurately, and to use exactly the amounts given in the instructions. If you do not, the experiment may not work properly. When you are doing the same experiment on two different substances to compare them, make sure you use equal amounts of the substances, or the experiment will not be fair. Here are some ways to measure chemicals.

For lots of the experiments you can measure the chemicals in spoonfuls. A spoonful of dry substance should be rounded, not heaped.

To measure out equal amounts of liquids, use a jar. Mark a line anywhere on the jar with a felt-tip pen. To measure each liquid, fill the jar up to the line.

In some experiments the instructions tell you to measure the depth of the liquid in a jar. It does not matter how big your jar is.

Dissolving

To dissolve a substance in a liquid you have to stir it for several minutes, then leave it for a while and stir again.

When a substance dissolves, it disappears and becomes part of the liquid. Some substances never dissolve completely though.

Safety hints

All the experiments in this book are quite safe, and most of the chemicals are harmless. However, even harmless substances can be dangerous if you mix them wrongly, so always take great care and follow the instructions. Below there is a checklist of safety points to remember.

Never invent your own experiments, or play with chemicals. Always take care to follow instructions.

Label all chemicals clearly and keep them away from young children, on a high shelf or in a cupboard you can lock. You must be especially careful with chemicals such as copper sulphate, which is poisonous. Mark "HARMFUL" in big letters on the label.

Keep a set of equipment, such as knives and spoons, for use only in the experiments. Buy them specially if you cannot find old ones that are no longer used.

Never taste or eat chemicals and do not experiment near food. Try not to rub your eyes or bite your nails while doing experiments.

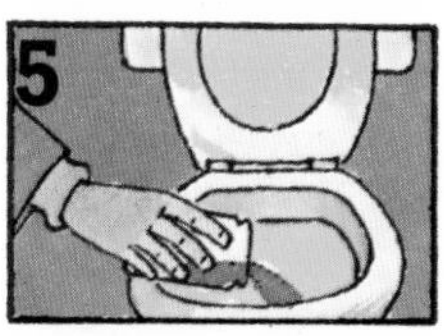

When you have finished an experiment, wash the chemicals away down the sink with plenty of water. If they are dangerous chemicals, flush them down the lavatory. Then wash your hands.

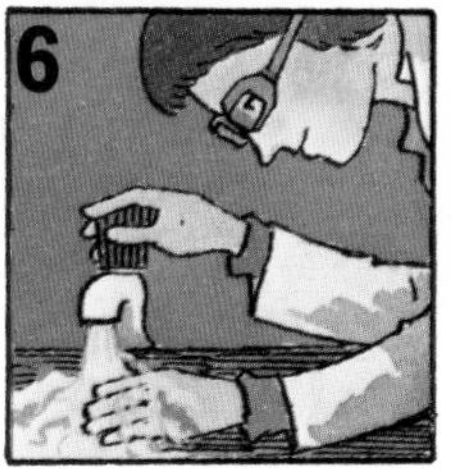

Some chemists wear goggles to prevent chemicals going in their eyes. If you do get something in your eye, or spill a chemical on your hands or clothes, wash it away with plenty of water.

If you ever do have an accident with chemicals, go to a doctor immediately and tell him or her the name of the chemical involved.

Acids at home

"Acid" is the name for a group of chemicals which share certain characteristics. Lots of the substances in your kitchen cupboard are acids. Most acids are sour. You will find out about some of their other characteristics as you do the experiments on the next few pages.

To find out which things are acids, you can test them with a liquid called an "indicator".

How to make an indicator

You can make an indicator from red cabbage.* Chop up about a quarter of a cabbage.

Put the pieces in a saucepan and add some boiling water – just enough to cover the cabbage.

Stir, then leave the pieces to soak for at least 15 minutes.

Now you need to separate the liquid from the cabbage. You can do this by filtering it, as shown on the opposite page.

Keep the filtered liquid in a bottle with a lid and label it. You will be using this indicator in lots of the experiments.

*If you cannot get red cabbage you can use rose petals (not white or yellow) or blackberries.

How to filter

1

Filtering is a way of straining a liquid to remove all the bits from it. Filtering removes even very fine particles from a liquid.

2

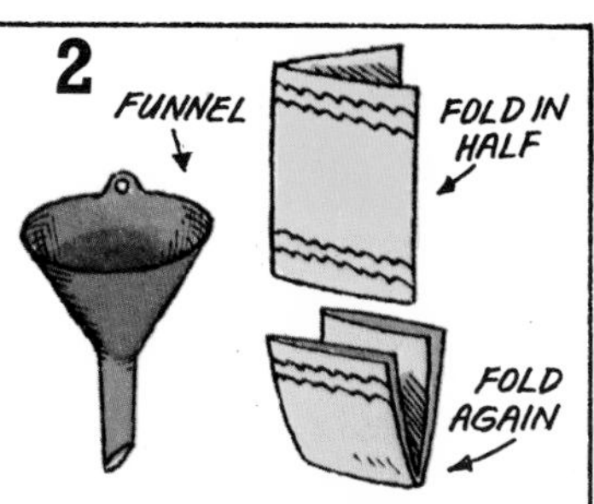

To make a filter you need a piece of kitchen paper towel and a funnel.* Fold the paper towel in half, then in half again, as shown.

3

Hold three corners of the paper together and pull the other corner out, like this. This makes a cone shape which fits in the funnel.

4

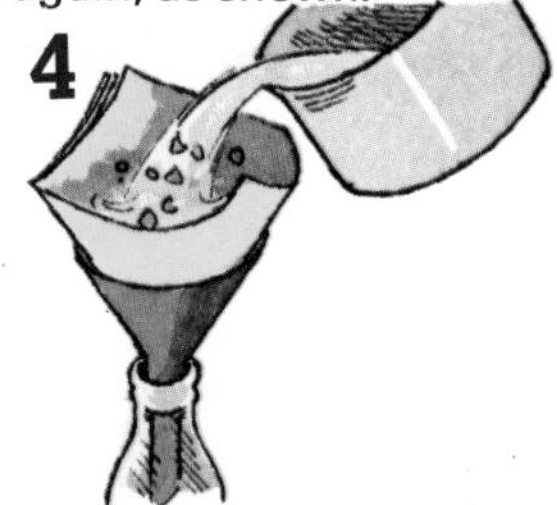

Put the funnel in a bottle and pour the liquid into the paper. The solid bits stay in the paper and the pure liquid drips through into the bottle.

Acid test

Now prepare some indicator for the acid test. Pour a little indicator into several jars and stick labels on all of them.

On one of the labels, write "CONTROL". You can find out how to do the test on the next page.

* *You can find out where to buy a funnel on page 61.*

Testing for acids

Now you can use the indicator, prepared on the previous page, to find out how many acids you have at home. Here is a list of ideas for things to test.

DARK LIQUIDS SUCH AS TEA WILL MAKE THE INDICATOR LOOK BROWN, SO ADD VERY LITTLE

Things to test

Lemon juice
Bicarbonate of soda
Baking powder
Vinegar
Cola drink
A boiled sweet
Washing-up liquid
Washing soda
Liquid floor cleaner
Orange juice
Sour milk
Indigestion tablets
Tea (without milk)
Milk of magnesia

How to do the test

To each jar of indicator, add a few drops (or bits) of one of the substances. Do not add anything to the control jar, though. Write the name of the substance on the label on the jar.

Now compare the colour of the liquid in each jar with the colour of the indicator in the "control" jar. If the liquid has turned pink, the substance tested is an acid.

If the liquid turns blue or green, the substance belongs to a different group of chemicals called "alkalis".* In some of the the jars it may take an hour or two for the colour to change.

*Petal indicator goes yellow and blackberry indicator goes blue or green.

More about acids and alkalis

Acids and alkalis are two different groups of chemicals. Most acids are sour, like lemon juice and vinegar. Strong acids, such as sulphuric acid are corrosive, that is, they eat away other materials. Some alkalis are also corrosive and can be just as dangerous as acids.

Did you know that the poison in a bee sting is an acid and the poison in a wasp sting is an alkali?

3

It is a good idea to write down which substances are acids and which are alkalis. Did you find any substances which were neither acid nor alkali?

Using a control

A control is a copy of the experiment, on which you do not do the tests. Chemists use a control so they can be sure the results are due to the test itself, and not to the equipment.

Making acids disappear

Here is an experiment to see what happens when you mix an acid and an alkali. For the acid you can use the juice of a lemon and for the alkali, some bicarbonate of soda. You need some red cabbage or blackberry indicator *

Squeeze the lemon and put the juice in a jar labelled "ACID". Put about 2cm of water in another jar and stir in two teaspoons of bicarbonate of soda. Label this jar "ALKALI".

Now pour a little of the alkali into a clean jar and test it with indicator. It should go green or blue. Keep this as a control.

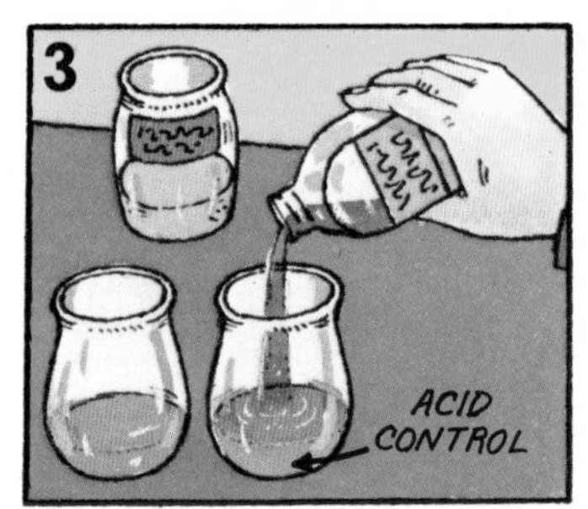

Pour some of the acid into two more jars. Add some indicator to both until they go pink. Put one jar on one side as a control.

Take the other jar of acid plus indicator and add a few drops of alkali to it, drop by drop. You could use an eyedropper.

As you add the alkali, the pink coloured liquid turns purple. This shows that the liquid is no longer an acid.

Rose petal indicator does not work for this experiment.

Where the acid goes

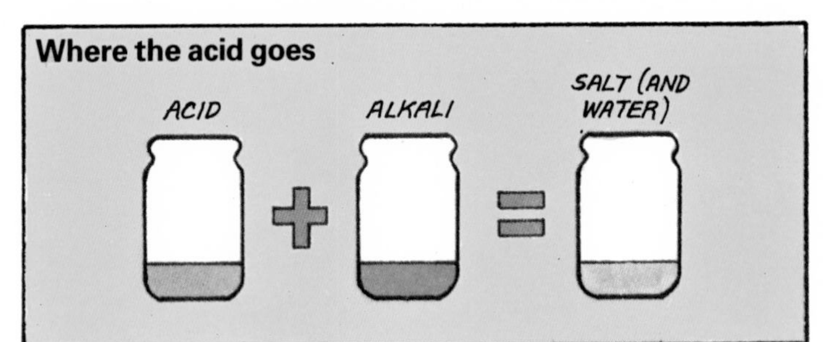

When you mix an acid and an alkali, they make a different kind of chemical, called a "salt". Most salts are neutral, that is, neither acidic nor alkaline. This is why the liquid changed back to the same colour as the indicator.

If it did not work

If your liquid went green, you added too much alkali. Try adding more acid to cancel out the extra alkali.

Neutralizing stomach aches

Indigestion can be caused by too much acid in the stomach. Indigestion pills and powders are alkaline, so they cancel out the acid.

More about salts

There are hundreds of different kinds of salts, including the salt we eat. This is called sodium chloride, and it is the result of the reaction between the alkali, sodium hydroxide and hydrochloric acid. These chemicals are very dangerous, but when they are mixed, they are neutralized and form a harmless salt.

Water tests

Tap water is not pure – it has lots of chemicals from the rocks in the ground dissolved in it. Here is a test to find out how these chemicals affect the water.

For the test you need some distilled water which has had all the chemicals taken out of it. Distilled water is used in car batteries, so you may have some at home, or you can buy it from a garage or chemist.

You also need three jars with lids, an eyedropper* and some soap flakes, made by grating a bar of soap.

In one of the jars, make some soap solution by dissolving a tablespoonful of soap flakes in six tablespoons of hot water.

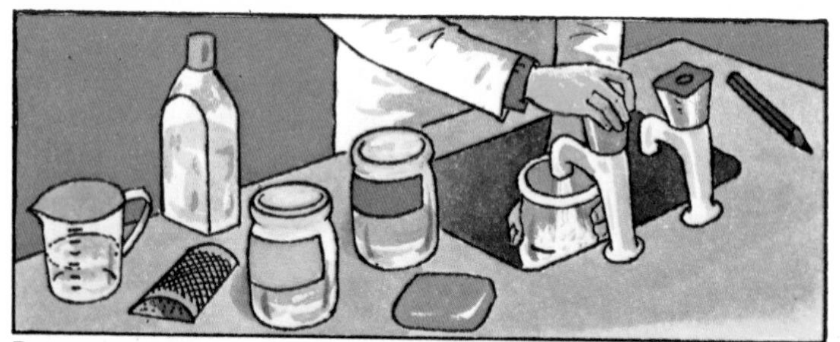

Put some tap water in one jar and the same amount of distilled water in another jar. Label the jars.

To make sure you have equal amounts put a line on a third jar and use that to measure out the distilled and tap water.

 You can find out where to buy an eyedropper on page 61.

Doing the test

With the eyedropper, add five drops of soap solution to the jar of distilled water.

Put the lid on and shake the jar to see if the soap lathers. If it does not, add five more drops of soap and shake it again. Go on adding soap until it lathers and note how many drops it takes.

Now do the same test on the jar of tap water. Count how many drops of soap it needs to make a lather. If it needs a lot, add the drops 10 or 20 at a time.

Which water needed the most soap to lather? Water which needs a lot of soap is said to be "hard". If it lathers with very little soap, it is said to be "soft".

What makes water hard

In the test, the tap water should need more soap than the distilled water, because the chemicals in tap water make it difficult for soap to lather.

The chemicals in tap water are calcium salts. When you add soap the calcium part of the salts reacts with the soap and makes scum. The soap will not lather until all the calcium in the water is used up. Over the page you can find out how to make hard water soft.

Making hard water soft

The tap water in some parts of the country is much harder than in others. This is because it has flowed over rocks which contain calcium salts. Here is an experiment to make hard water soft. You need tap water, washing soda and soap solution from the previous experiment.

Measure the same amount of tap water as you used in the last experiment into a jar. Add a teaspoonful of washing soda and stir until it has all dissolved.

When the washing soda has dissolved, add some drops of soap.* Shake the jar as before and see how many drops it needs to make a lather.

You should find that the water needs much less soap to make a lather than in the previous experiment. The washing soda has made the hardness disappear.

How washing soda works

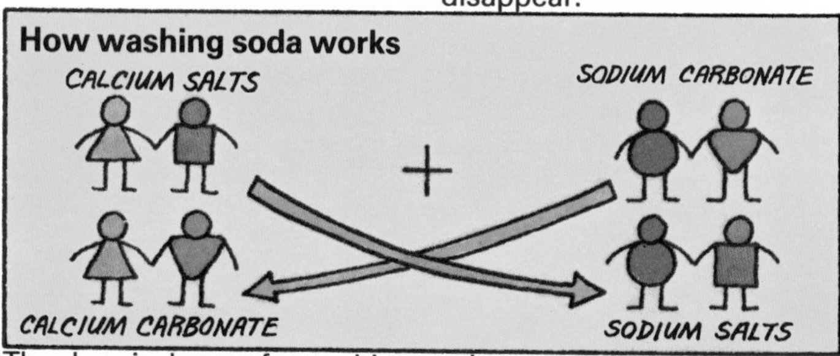

The chemical name for washing soda is sodium carbonate. The carbonate part of the washing soda joins up with the calcium in hard water and makes a new substance called calcium carbonate. The calcium is no longer able to react with the soap, so the soap can lather more easily.

**If your soap solution solidifies, add more hot water.*

Another water test

Now put some boiled tap water (the same amount as in previous tests) in a jar and let it cool. Add drops of soap.

Shake the jar and add more drops until the soap lathers. Does the boiled water need less soap than unboiled tap water?

What boiling does

If the boiled water needed less soap to lather, the water is temporary hard water.* This has a calcium salt in it called calcium hydrogen carbonate. When the water boils, this calcium salt splits into calcium carbonate and carbon dioxide gas. The calcium carbonate sinks to the bottom and does not stop the soap lathering.

Calcium carbonate forms the substance in the kettle known as "fur". The carbon dioxide escapes in the steam.

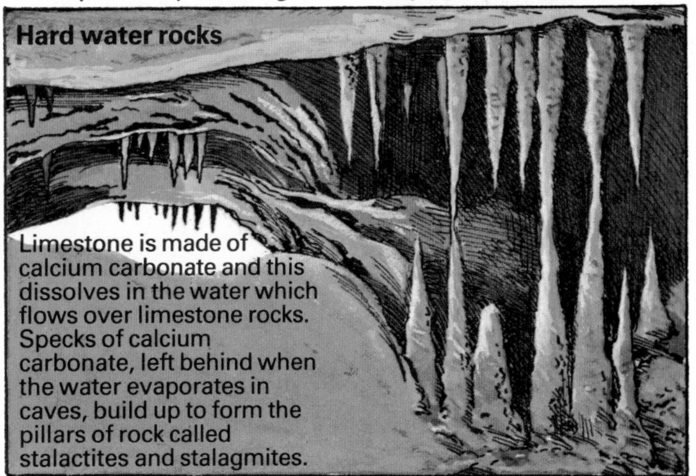

Hard water rocks

Limestone is made of calcium carbonate and this dissolves in the water which flows over limestone rocks. Specks of calcium carbonate, left behind when the water evaporates in caves, build up to form the pillars of rock called stalactites and stalagmites.

**If boiling makes no difference to hard water, it is permanent hard water.*

How to make bath salts

Bath salts make bath water soft and soapy, and stop the soap making a scum. The water tests in the last few experiments showed how washing soda makes water soft, and you can use washing soda to make bath salts.

As well as washing soda, you need some food colouring, some cologne or perfume, a polythene bag, a rolling pin, a bowl and a jar to keep the bath salts in.

Put five tablespoons of washing soda in a polythene bag. Use the clear lumps of washing soda, not the powdery white ones near the top of the packet.

Break the lumps of washing soda into small pieces by rolling on the bag with the rolling pin.

Empty the washing soda into a bowl and add four or five drops of cologne or perfume, and some drops of food colouring.

Experiment
See what happens if you put some bath salts on a saucer and leave them in the air for a few days.

The bath salts go white and powdery, like the lumps of washing soda near the top of the packet. The crystals of washing soda contain water which escapes into the air, leaving the crystals white and powdery. So you should always keep the lid on your bath salts.

Stir in food colouring until all the washing soda is brightly coloured. Then tip it into a jar, screw on the lid and label it.

You could make several lots of bath salts using different food colourings, then mix them, or put them in layers in a jar.

Soap tests

On this page you can find out how soap works, then, opposite, you can do a test to see which make of washing powder works the best. Some washing powders are called detergents. They are not made from the same substances as soap, but they work in the same way.

For the tests you will need several different makes of washing powder,* a piece of rag, some butter or margarine, several jars and some kitchen scales.

Smear a thick lump of butter on a small piece of rag. Put the rag in a jar and add a teaspoonful of washing powder. Then gently pour in some warm water and watch what happens.

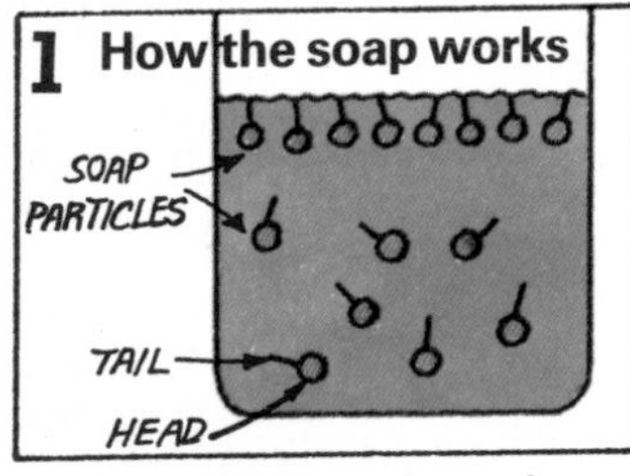

Each tiny particle of soap has a head end and a tail end. The head loves water and the tail hates water.

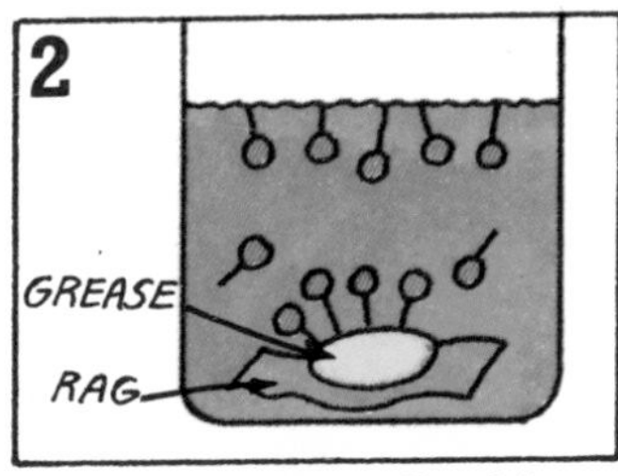

The water-hating tails of the soap bury themselves in the grease and the water-loving heads stay in the water.

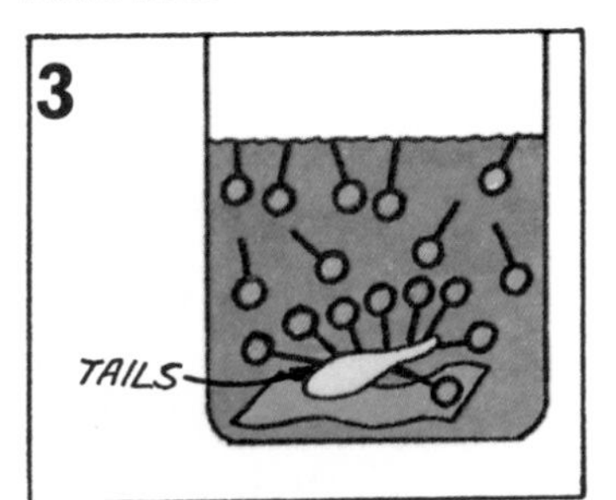

More and more tails try to get into the grease, and they work their way between the grease and the cloth.

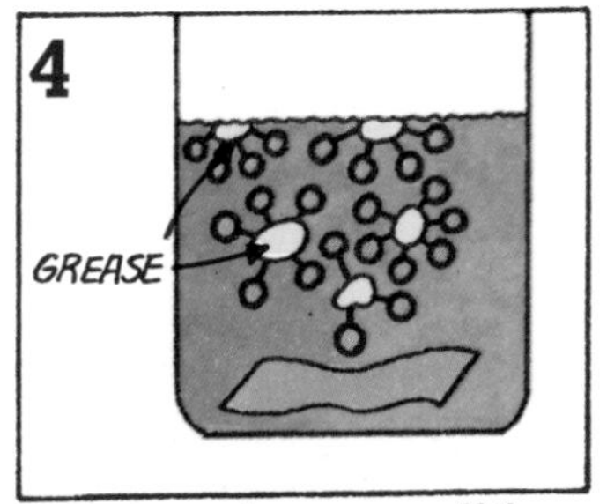

They force the grease off the cloth and break it up into tiny balls. You could probably see this happening in the soap test.

 *You could see if your neighbours have different kinds and will let

Which powder works best?

Most washing powder manufacturers claim that their brand of powder washes whiter and cleaner than all the others. Here is a scientific way to test the powders.

For this test you need several different kinds of washing powder, some kitchen scales and a very dirty, greasy piece of rag. You could make the rag greasy by wiping it on a bicycle chain.

Weigh out 25g of each powder and put each one in a separate labelled jar.

Add the same amount of hot water to each jar to dissolve the powders.

Put a small piece of greasy rag into each jar. Stir each 15 times and leave to soak overnight.

Rinse each rag separately and put it back near its jar. Be careful not to mix them up.

Now examine the pieces of rag and see which is the cleanest. You could make a chart showing which powders worked best, and how much they cost for 25g (divide packet price by total number of grammes, then multiply by 25).

Another test

Try testing each powder (dissolved in hot water) with red cabbage indicator to see if it is acid or alkaline.

Alkaline powders are not good for woollen fabrics and acid powders can be harmful to nylon.

you have a small amount.

Soap powder eats egg experiment

For this experiment you will need some "biological" washing powder. This kind of powder has a special chemical in it which removes dirt by "eating" it. You can find out how in the experiment. You will also need some ordinary washing powder and an egg. To check if a powder is "biological", look on the packet for the words "acts biologically" or "digests dirt".

1 Boil the egg for 10 minutes, so it is hard-boiled. Let it cool, then peel it.

2 Put a tablespoonful of each powder into two separate jars and label them.

3 Then put about 125ml (or eight tablespoons) warm water into each jar.

4 Cut two pieces of egg white, both the same size, and put them in the jars. Put the jars somewhere warm (near a radiator or in an airing cupboard) and leave them for two days

Two days later

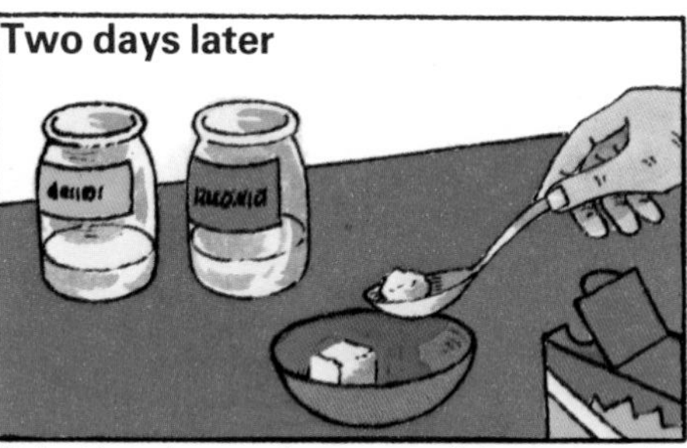

Take the pieces of egg out of the jars and examine them. You should find that the egg from the biological powder is now smaller than the piece from the ordinary powder.

How it works

The special chemical in the biological powder is called an "enzyme". The enzyme attacks the particles of egg and breaks them into smaller particles which dissolve in water. The egg in the other powder shows that egg does not dissolve in ordinary soapy water, and that it is the enzyme which "eats" the egg away.

5

If you cannot find somewhere warm, wrap the jars and put near a hot pipe.

Enzymes in your stomach

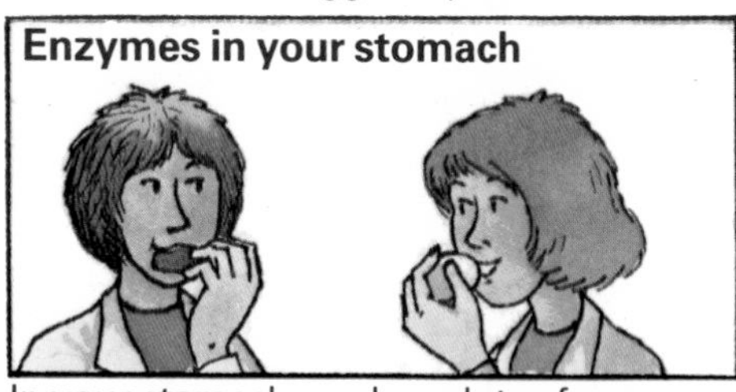

In your stomach you have lots of enzymes attacking the food you eat and breaking it up, just like the washing powder enzyme. The enzymes in your stomach break the food into molecules which can dissolve in your blood.

Food tests

Our bodies need lots of different substances to keep them healthy, and we get these substances from the food we eat. One of these substances is called starch.

Here is a test to find out which foods contain starch. You need an eyedropper, a jar, newspaper and a chemical called iodine* which changes colour when you mix it with starch.

COVER TABLE WITH NEWSPAPER

EYEDROPPER

Pour a little iodine into the jar, then add the same amount of water to dilute it. Iodine stains, so be careful not to spill it.

Doing the test

Now you can use the iodine to see which foods contain starch. Below there is a list of ideas for things to test.

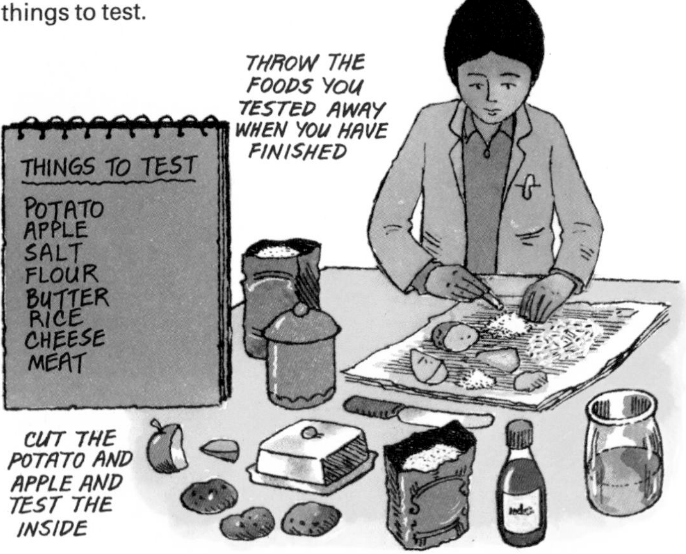

Put a small piece of each type of food on the newspaper. Then, with the eyedropper, put a drop of iodine on to each of them and watch what happens.

If the iodine turns blue-black, or dark brown, it means the food contains starch. Note which foods contain starch. Do they have anything in common?

 *You can buy this from a chemist. Ask for red tincture of iodine.

Which foods contain starch

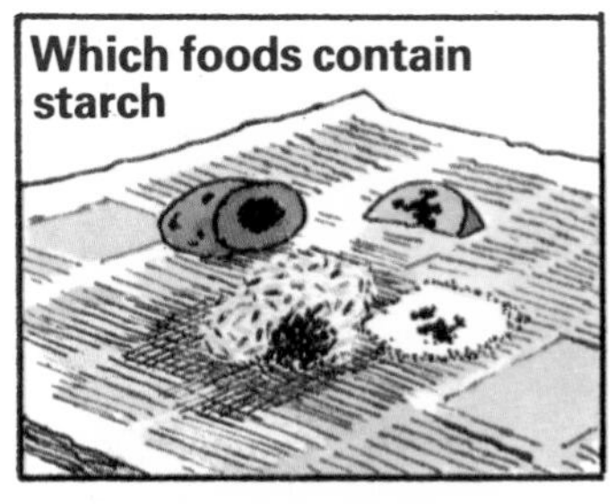

In the test, you probably found that only things which come from plants contain starch.

Starch is a substance made by plants, and we get the starch we need by eating food made from plants.

1 Spit test

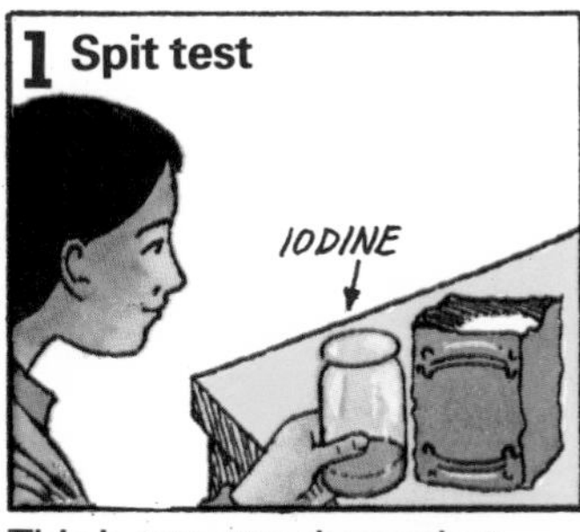

This is a test to show what happens to starch when we eat it. You need some flour,iodine solution and a large mug.

Put a teaspoon of flour in a mug, add a little water and stir to make a paste. Then fill the mug with boiling water and stir.

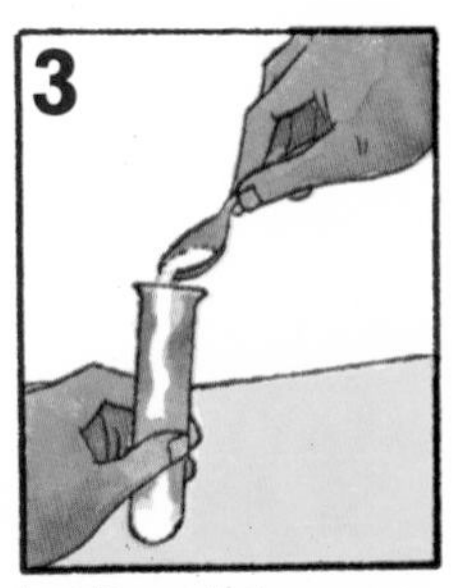

Let it cool, then put a teaspoonful of the flour solution in a test-tube.

Pour one drop of the solution from the test-tube into a saucer or jar lid.

Then test the drop of solution with iodine to see if it contains starch.

Turn over ▶

Now spit several times into the test-tube. Cover the top of the tube and shake it to mix the flour solution and spit.

Put the test-tube in a warm place. Every 20 minutes, pour out one drop, test it with iodine and see what colour the iodine goes.

What happens

After several hours you should find that the iodine no longer changes colour, or only changes very slightly.

This shows that there is very little starch left in the solution. It has been "eaten" by the spit. You can find out how below.

What spit does

The proper name for spit is saliva, and it contains an enzyme, like the washing powder on pages 24-25.* Starch molecules are too big to be absorbed by our bodies and the enzyme in saliva breaks them up into the smaller molecules of a different substance called maltose.

In the spit test, the starch in the flour was changed to maltose, and this is why the iodine no longer changed colour.

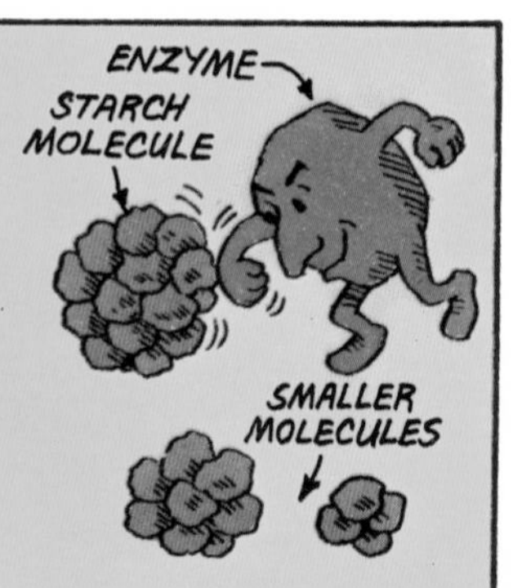

It is not the same enzyme as in the washing powder.

More starch tests

Try testing white paper, paper glue and laundry starch (dissolved in hot water) with iodine, and see what happens.

The iodine should turn blue-black or brown, showing that these things contain starch.The starch is extracted from plants and treated to make a gluey substance which is used in paper glue and in laundry starch, and for making paper.

Papermaking

A film of starch solution is often put on paper to hold the fibres of the paper together and give it a smooth surface.

Laundry starch

In the same way, laundry starch forms a thin film on a fabric and helps to stiffen it and give it a smooth surface.

Make your own glue

If you need some glue, but have run out, you can make some from flour and water. This glue is very good for sticking paper. People used to make wallpaper paste like this, but it tended to stain the paper and sometimes went mouldy.

To make the glue, mix a tablespoon of flour with a few drops of cold water to make a paste. Then stir in eight tablespoons of boiling water.

Do not keep the glue too long, or it will go mouldy.

What is gas?

Gas is the name for a group of airlike chemicals. There are lots of different kinds of gases. Most of them are invisible, but some gases have a smell. For instance, the gas hydrogen sulphide smells of bad eggs and is sometimes used to make stink bombs. Never sniff a gas though, as some are deadly poisonous.

On the next few pages you can make a gas and test it to find out what it is.

Air is a mixture of gases. The main ones are oxygen, which our bodies need to stay alive, and nitrogen.

You can sometimes see gas as bubbles in a liquid. The bubbles in a goldfish bowl are made by the gas the fish breathe out.

The bubbles in fizzy drinks are also a gas and the drink goes flat as the gas escapes.

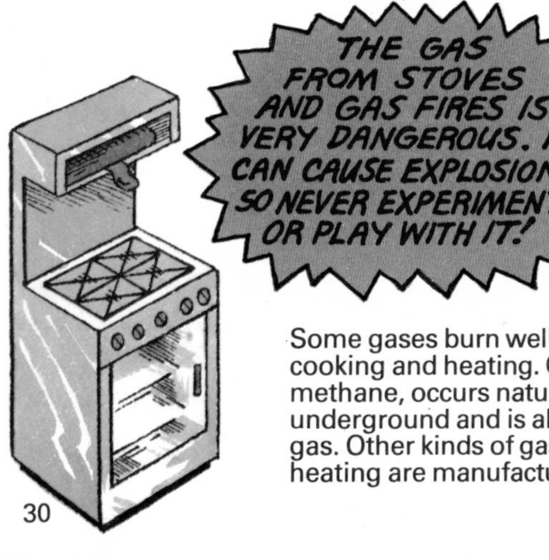

Some gases burn well and are used for cooking and heating. One of these, called methane, occurs naturally in rocks underground and is also known as natural gas. Other kinds of gas for cooking and heating are manufactured from coal or oil.

Making a gas

You can make a gas from washing soda and vinegar, as shown on the right. Try this, then make the equipment to catch the gas, so you can test it to find out what it is. The gas test is on the next page.

You need some washing soda and vinegar, a test-tube, plastic tubing,* plasticine and a liquid called limewater. You can buy limewater from some chemists, or make it as shown on page 59.

To make the gas, pour 2cm vinegar into a small jar and add four or five lumps of washing soda. The mixture bubbles and fizzes as the gas escapes from it.

1 Gas-catching equipment

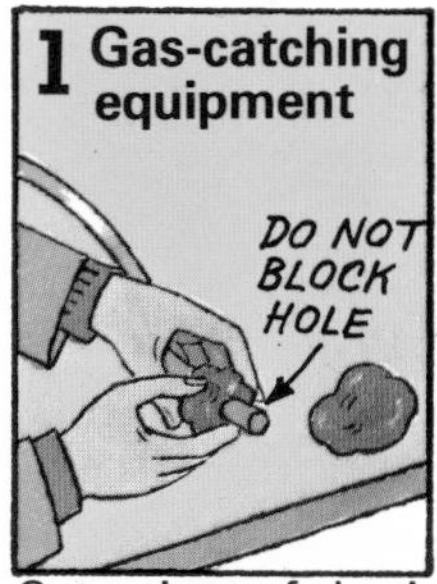

Cut a piece of plastic tubing about 40cm long and wrap plasticine round one end.

2

Push the end with the plasticine into the test-tube. It should fit tightly like a cork. If it is loose, take it out and add more plasticine.

3

Now prepare the equipment for the test on the next page. Pull the bung out of the test-tube and have some vinegar and washing soda ready.

4

LIMEWATER

Pour a small amount of limewater into a clean jar or test-tube. The limewater should be about 0.5cm deep.

See page 61 for where to buy plastic tubing and page 58 for another way to make gas-catching equipment.

Testing the gas

Now you can test the gas made from washing soda and vinegar using the equipment shown on the previous page. You have to do the test quickly or the gas escapes, so read the instructions right through before you start.

Fill the test-tube one third full with vinegar and add four or five lumps of washing soda.

Then, as fast as you can, push the plasticine bung in the test-tube and hold the free end of the tubing in the limewater.

The gas should bubble out of the tube in the limewater. If nothing happens the bung may be leaking. Add more plasticine.

The mixture should go on making gas for about two minutes. Look carefully at the limewater. As the gas bubbles through it, the limewater should go cloudy.

What the test shows

Limewater goes cloudy when the gas carbon dioxide is bubbled through it. So the gas made by mixing vinegar and washing soda must be carbon dioxide. You can find out what happens in this chemical reaction on the next page.

If your limewater did not go cloudy, try shaking it. If it still does not work, test the limewater as shown on page 59, to make sure it is the right kind.

Another gas to test

You can try the limewater test on your breath. Dip one end of a drinking straw into some fresh limewater. Blow through it for two or three minutes and watch what happens to the limewater. What does this tell you about your breath?

More gas-making experiments

Here are some more things you can mix to make a gas. Take anything from list A and mix it with something from list B. Each time, bubble the gas through limewater, as shown on the previous page, to see if it is carbon dioxide.

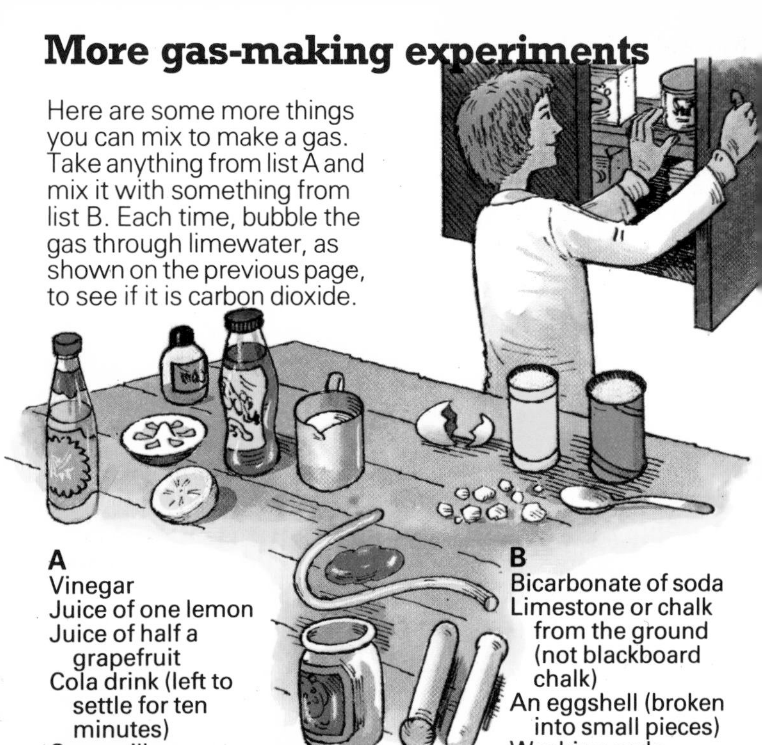

A
- Vinegar
- Juice of one lemon
- Juice of half a grapefruit
- Cola drink (left to settle for ten minutes)
- Sour milk

B
- Bicarbonate of soda
- Limestone or chalk from the ground (not blackboard chalk)
- An eggshell (broken into small pieces)
- Washing soda

How the gas is made

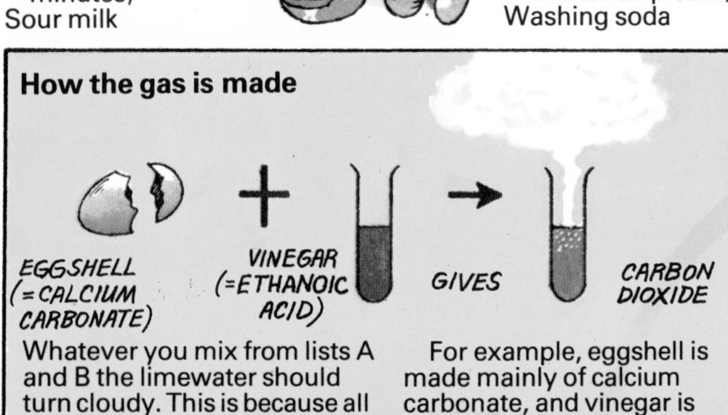

Whatever you mix from lists A and B the limewater should turn cloudy. This is because all the things in list A are acids and all the things in list B are substances called carbonates. When you mix an acid with a carbonate, they react and make carbon dioxide.

For example, eggshell is made mainly of calcium carbonate, and vinegar is ethanoic acid. All carbonates contain carbon and oxygen. When you mix a carbonate with an acid, the carbon and oxygen escape as carbon dioxide gas.

More about carbon dioxide

Carbon dioxide is one of the gases in air and, as the test on the previous page shows, when we breathe out, our breath contains carbon dioxide. There is only a tiny amount of carbon dioxide in the air though (about 0.03%).

Plants absorb carbon dioxide through their leaves and use it to make food. Plants give off oxygen, so they help to keep a good supply of oxygen in the air, and they use up carbon dioxide.

Dry ice

Carbon dioxide can be made into a solid substance called "dry ice" which is much colder than ordinary ice. It is used in frozen food factories.

Smoke in plays is usually made from dry ice. When dry ice is plunged into boiling water the carbon dioxide evaporates and makes a white mist.

Fire extinguishers

Carbon dioxide is good for fire-fighting and many fire-extinguishers contain compressed carbon dioxide. Things need oxygen to burn and when carbon dioxide is sprayed on a fire it pushes away the oxygen and so suffocates the flames.

Making fizzy drinks

The bubbles of gas in fizzy drinks are carbon dioxide. You can check this by fitting gas-catching equipment to a bottle of fizzy drink and testing the gas with limewater, as shown on page 32.

You can make still drinks fizzy with a special powder made from bicarbonate of soda, citric acid crystals and icing sugar. Follow the instructions given below and use kitchen, not chemistry, utensils.

1

Put six teaspoons of citric acid crystals and three teaspoons of bicarbonate of soda into a bowl.

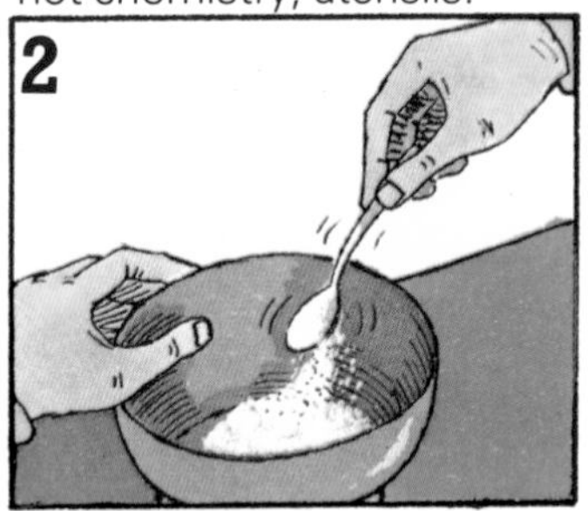

Then, with the back of the spoon, grind the two substances against the side of the bowl to make a fine powder.

Stir in two tablespoons of icing sugar. Then pour the mixture into a clean, dry jar with a screw-cap. Label it "FIZZ POWDER".

To make a fizzy drink, put two teaspoons of powder in a glass and fill it up with a still drink, such as orange or lime-juice.*

**If the drink tastes sour add more sugar to your powder.*

How it works

In the drink, the citric acid crystals dissolve and make citric acid. This reacts with the carbonate in bicarbonate of soda and makes carbon dioxide gas. The gas bubbles through the drink and makes it fizz.

When the reaction is over there is no more carbon dioxide and the drink goes flat. The sugar takes away the sour taste of the citric acid and bicarbonate of soda.

How to make sherbet

You can use the same ingredients to make sherbet powder. Grind six teaspoons of citric acid crystals and three of bicarbonate of soda together as before, then stir in four tablespoons of icing sugar. Keep the sherbet powder in a jar with a screw-on lid.

When you lick the sherbet, the citric acid crystals dissolve and react with the bicarbonate of soda to make carbon dioxide gas. The fizz you feel on your tongue is the bubbles of gas.

Chemical muddle puzzle

You can solve this puzzle by doing chemical tests. You need some flour, salt, icing sugar, cream of tartar, and bicarbonate of soda.

Chef Zabor is in a muddle. He has put his baking ingredients, flour, icing sugar, bicarbonate of soda, cream of tartar and salt, into jars and forgotten to label them. Now he needs a chemist to help sort out which is which.

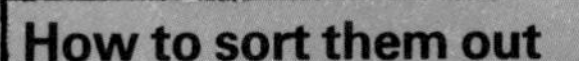

How to sort them out

Clues

1. Cream of tartar is acid.
2. Flour and sugar are neutral.
3. Flour is the only one that does not dissolve.
4. Table salt* and bicarbonate of soda are alkaline.
5. Bicarbonate of soda is a carbonate, so it makes carbon dioxide when mixed with an acid.

The clues above show the chemical characteristics, or properties, of each of the baking ingredients. To sort out the powders you need to test them, as shown opposite, to find out which are acid, which dissolve and so on.

Then you can identify the powders by checking the results of the tests against the clues. For example, the powder that is neutral and does not dissolve must be flour. Check your results with the answers on page 61.

Salt is really neutral, but table salt contains a substance which makes it alkaline.

Tests

1. Find out whether the powders are acid, alkaline or neutral, by doing the indicator test described on page 12.
2. Add warm water to each powder, stir and leave for a few minutes to see if it dissolves.
3. Mix each of the powders with an acid, such as vinegar, and do the gas test on page 32 to see if it makes carbon dioxide.

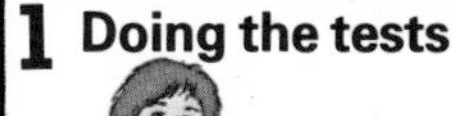

1 Doing the tests

Ask someone to put two teaspoons* of each ingredient into unlabelled jars, while you are not looking.

Label the jars A, B, C, D, E. Then label five test-tubes (or five more jars) A-E. Always test powder A in tube or jar A.

Use only a little of each powder in each test.* Wash the test-tubes out between tests.

Make a chart and fill in the results of each test. When you have done all the tests you will know the chemical properties of each powder. To identify them, match the properties with the clues given opposite.

**Use a clean teaspoon for each powder.*

Testing inks and dyes

Inks and dyes are made from coloured chemicals. To make all the different colours, lots of different coloured chemicals are mixed together, like mixing paints.

Here are some tests to separate the chemicals in felt-tip pens and sweets, so you can see all the different colours.

Ink blob test

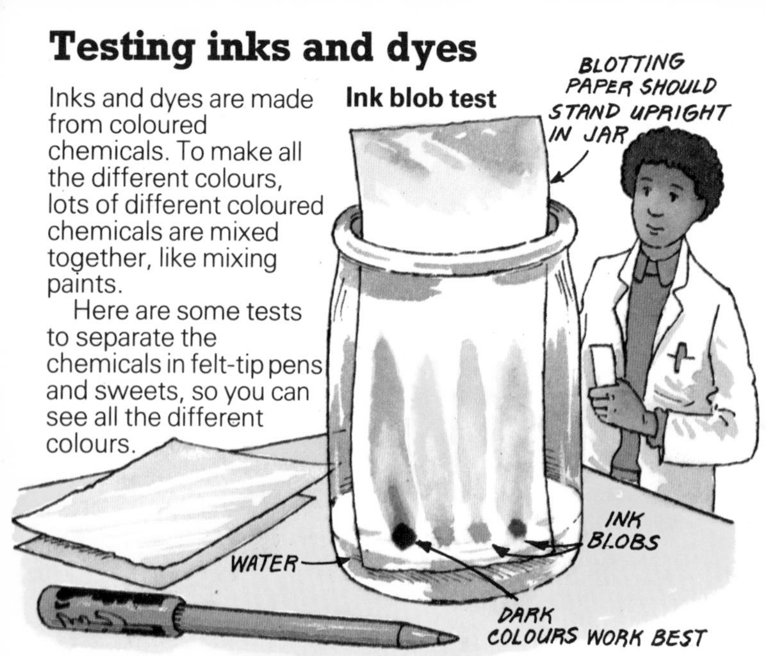

For this test you need some blotting paper, felt-tip pens and a jar with about 2cm of water in. Cut the blotting paper to make a strip just wide enough to fit in the jar. Then, about 5cm from one end, make blobs of colour with the felt-tip pens.

Put the paper in the jar, with the ink blobs at the bottom, and watch for about five minutes to see what happens. As the paper soaks up water, the blobs of ink separate into the different coloured chemicals of which they are made.

How it works

As the water rises up the blotting paper it dissolves the chemicals and carries them up with it. Some chemicals are more easily absorbed by the blotting paper than others, so they travel up it at different speeds. As the different chemicals separate, you can see the different colours. Some colours, such as red and yellow, are made from only one chemical, so they do not separate.

DIFFERENT COLOURED CHEMICALS

Testing food colours

You can do the same test on coloured, sugar-coated sweets (such as "Smarties") to see how many different chemicals are used to colour them. The black or brown sweets work best.

Put three sweets, all the same colour, on a saucer and add three or four drops of water.

Turn the sweets over and over so all the colour runs off into the water.

Cut a long, thin strip of blotting paper and dip one end into the coloured water.

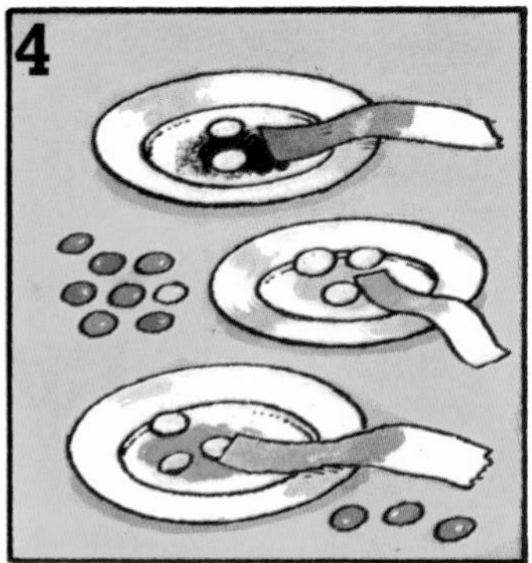

Leave the blotting paper in the water for about five minutes and watch what happens. Then try the test with different coloured sweets.

How it works

The coloured chemicals from the sweets are absorbed by the blotting paper in the same way as the chemicals in the inks. As they are absorbed at different rates, the chemicals separate and you can see the different colours.

Separating chemicals like this, by absorbing them, is called "chromatography". Over the page there is another chromatography experiment.

Detecting forgeries

The crook in the picture on the right is tampering with the figures on a cheque. He is changing the sum from 60 to 60,000 by adding noughts. You could prove the noughts were forged with a different pen, by doing a chromatography test.*

Here is an experiment to show how the test would work. You need two, different, black felt-tip pens, blotting paper and a jar with about 2cm of water in.

Cut a piece of blotting paper just wide enough to fit in the jar.

About 5cm from the bottom of the paper, write the figure 60 with one of the pens.

With the other pen, add three noughts to the figure to make 60,000.

Now put the blotting paper in the jar and watch what happens.

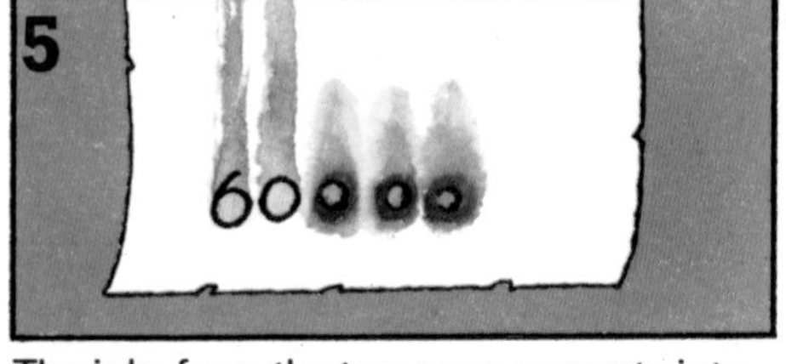

The inks from the two pens separate into the different coloured chemicals of which they are made. Different manufacturers use different chemicals in their inks, so the pattern of colours from the two pens is not the same and you can see that the noughts were added with a different pen.

**You can find out about chromatography on the previous page.*

Invisible ink experiments

Invisible inks are made from colourless chemicals which, when you burn them, or treat them with other chemicals, react and become coloured.

Here and on the next two pages there are two different ways of making invisible ink. The lemon juice ink on this page is easier than the one in the next experiment, so try this one first.

1 Lemon juice ink

For this ink you need the juice of a lemon, a piece of paper and a thin paintbrush to write with.

2 Write a message with the lemon juice, dipping the brush in the juice between each letter. Leave to dry for at least an hour, or until the writing is invisible.

3 To reveal the message put the paper, face down, on a shelf in the oven. Set the oven at 175°C (350°F), or gas mark 4, and leave for ten minutes.

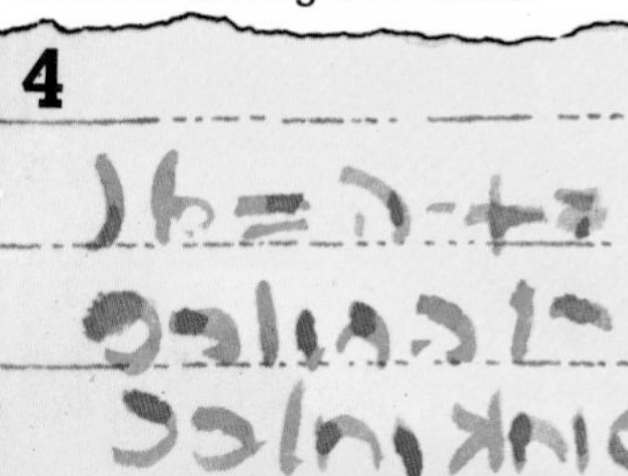

4 When you take the paper out of the oven, you should be able to see the writing quite clearly. Remember to turn the oven off.

How it works

The lemon juice burns in the heat of the oven, but the oven is not hot enough to burn the paper. Burning is a chemical reaction which changes the lemon juice and makes it go brown. So the letters of the message appear as brown marks of burnt lemon juice.

Another invisible ink

Here is another way to make invisible ink, using a special chemical which turns pink when you "develop" it with washing soda solution. It is quite difficult to do this and the ink may not work first time, so keep trying.

The chemical for the ink is called phenolphthalein.* This is used in some makes of laxative pills which you can buy from a chemist. Check on the packet that the pills do contain this chemical. You also need some washing soda and a paintbrush.

You need to use five or six of the pills. If they have a coloured coating, scrape it off with a knife.

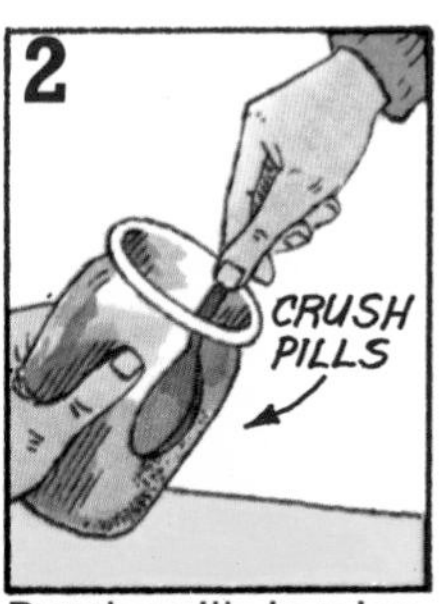

Put the pills in a jar and crush them to a fine powder with the back of a spoon.

Fill the jar about 3cm deep with warm water and stir to dissolve the powder.

Write a message with the paintbrush dipping it inthe "ink" between each stroke. Then leave it to dry.

Something to try

To conceal the secret message, you can write another letter on top. Use a ball-point pen which will not run when you develop the invisible ink.

Did you know?

In the past, prisoners of war made invisible ink from sweat and saliva. Like lemon juice, these become visible when you burn them.

 Pronounced fee-nol-thay-leen.

Developing the ink

With a clean teaspoon, put four teaspoons of washing soda in four tablespoons of hot water and stir until it has all dissolved.

Put about two teaspoons of warm water on a plate. Lay the paper with the message on the plate, so the paper absorbs the water.

Now, very carefully put drops of washing soda solution on the paper with a teaspoon. Try and spread each drop out as it falls on the paper. You may have to practise this to get it right.

When you add the washing soda, the letters of the secret message should appear bright pink. The letters do not last very long though, as the colour runs into the washing soda solution.

How it works

Phenolphthalein is an indicator, like the red cabbage water which you used to test for acids and alkalis. When you mix phenolphthalein with an alkali, such as washing soda, it turns pink.

How to split water

Water is made from two chemicals joined together. The chemicals are called oxygen and hydrogen. In this experiment you can split water into oxygen and hydrogen with the electric current from a battery.

Oxygen and hydrogen belong to a group of chemicals called "elements" from which all substances are made. You can find out more about elements over the page.

You need two pencils sharpened at both ends, a 9 volt battery, 15 amp fuse wire, a jar of water, scissors, paper and sticky tape.

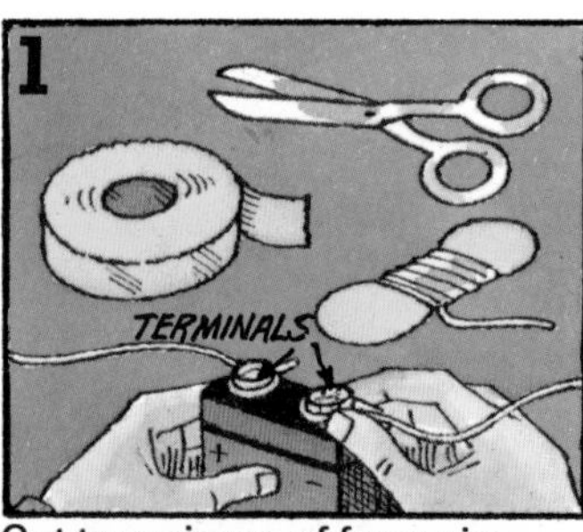

Cut two pieces of fuse wire about 20cm long and wind them round the metal terminals of the battery. Fix them with sticky tape.

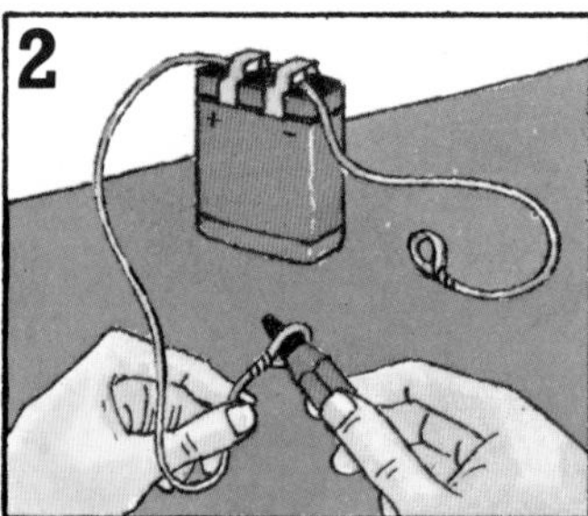

At the other end of each wire make a loop just big enough to fit round the lead point of a pencil.

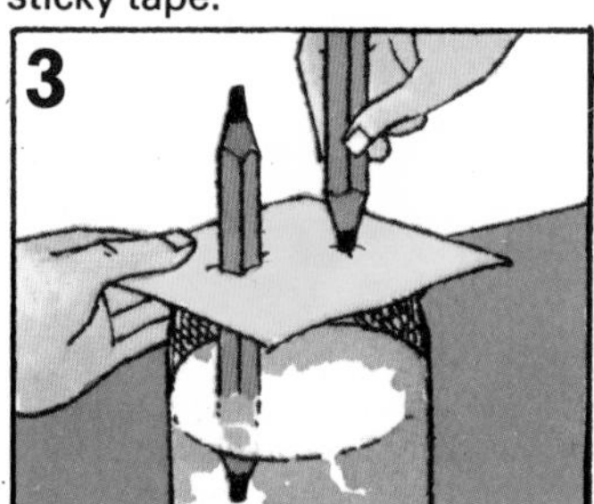

Rest a square of paper on the jar of water. Then push the pencils through it so they are held with their points in the water.

Loop the wires on to the lead points of the pencils. Then watch the pencil points in the water to see what happens.

What happens

When you connect the battery wires to the pencil leads, the electric current from the battery flows along the wires and pencil leads and through the water.

As the current flows you should see bubbles forming round the points of the pencils. These are bubbles of oxygen and hydrogen gas. You can tell which bubbles are hydrogen and which are oxygen by looking at the battery terminals.

The oxygen collects round the pencil attached to the positive terminal (marked "+"). The hydrogen collects round the pencil attached to the negative terminal (marked "–"). Which pencil has the most bubbles round it?

How it works

WATER MOLECULES

All substances are made of minute particles called atoms, and the atoms cling together in groups called molecules. Each water molecule contains two hydrogen atoms and one oxygen atom.

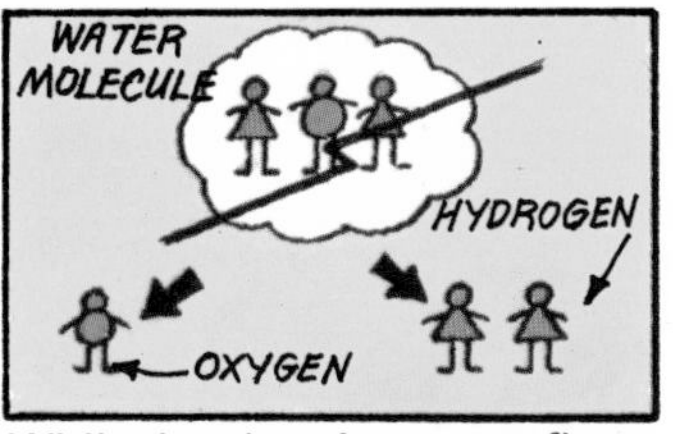

While the electric current flows the water molecules split up into atoms of hydrogen and oxygen. More hydrogen bubbles form because in water there are twice as many hydrogen atoms as oxygen.

What are elements?

Elements are the basic chemicals from which all substances are made. There are only about 100 elements and all the millions of substances on Earth are made from different combinations of them.

A substance made from a combination of elements is called a compound. For example water is a compound and in the experiment on the previous page, you split it into hydrogen and oxygen, the elements of which it is made.

Some elements are well-known substances, such as gold, silver oxygen and carbon. Others are rare chemicals that are hardly ever seen.

Most of the things in this picture, including the human body, are made from compounds of only six different elements. Almost all the substances in the human body are made from different combinations of the elements oxygen, carbon, nitrogen, hydrogen, calcium and phosphorus. Hair, skin, muscles, wool and leather are all made from only four elements: oxygen, hydrogen, carbon and nitrogen.

What ancient chemists thought

The Ancient Greeks thought there were only four elements: earth, air, fire and water, and that everything else in the world was made from these four things.

Later, in the Middle Ages, people called alchemists believed they could turn ordinary metals to gold with a substance called the Philosopher's Stone. In their attempts to make the Stone they discovered a lot about the composition of different substances. They believed that sulphur, mercury and salt were the only three elements, and they wrote "recipes" for the Stone, using symbols for the elements and metals, as shown in the picture above.

Modern chemistry symbols

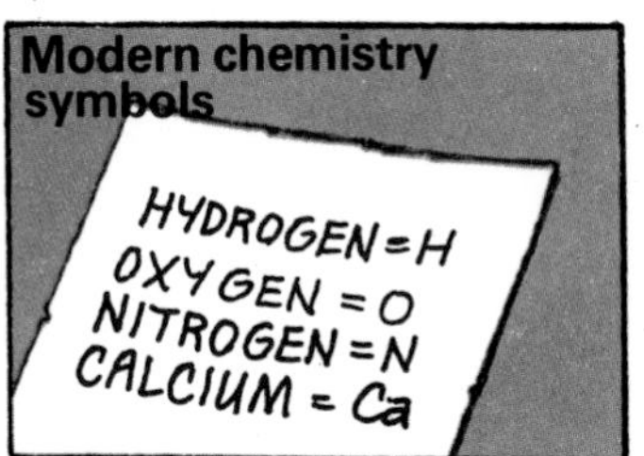

Chemists still use symbols for the elements. These are often the first letter or letters of the element's name. Chemists all over the world use the same symbols.

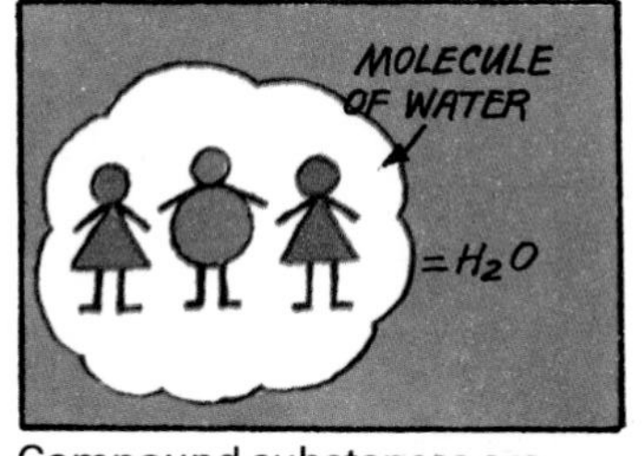

Compound substances are represented by the symbols of the elements they contain. So water is H_2O. The figure two shows there are two hydrogen atoms in each water molecule.

Sorting out elements

Elements can be divided into two groups: metals, such as gold, iron and tin, and non-metals, such as hydrogen, oxygen and sulphur. The metal elements share certain characteristics. They can be polished to make them shine, they conduct electricity (that is, electricity can flow through them) and they are good conductors of heat. These qualities make them useful for lots of different purposes, as shown in these pictures.

The shiny surface of mirrors is made with a thin layer of silver on the back of the glass.

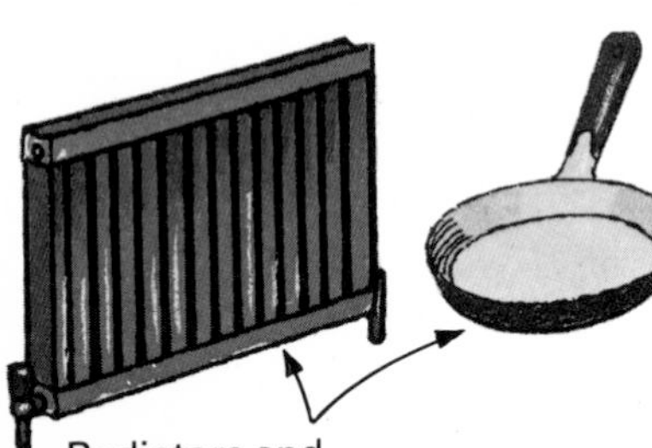

Radiators and cooking pans need to conduct heat, so they are made of metal.

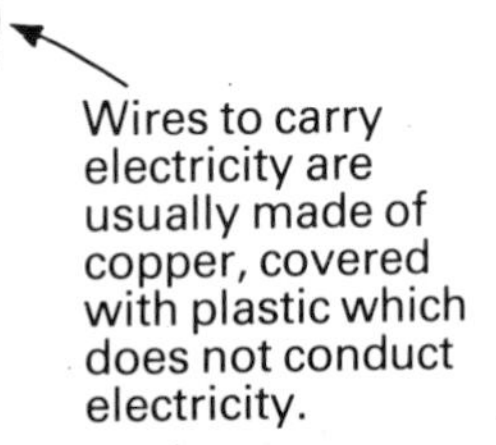

Wires to carry electricity are usually made of copper, covered with plastic which does not conduct electricity.

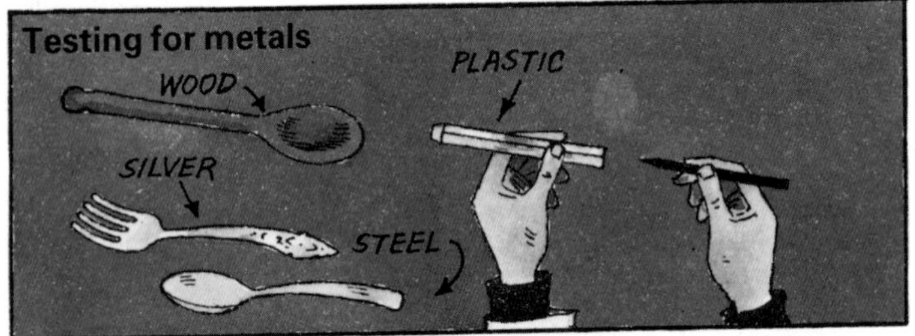

You can usually tell when substances are metals, but some are not so easy to recognize. On the next few pages you can see how chemists identify metals by testing them to see if they conduct heat and electricity. For the tests you need some long thin objects, such as the things shown above, made from several different substances.

Bean test for heat

This is a test which shows how well different substances conduct heat. You need things, such as those shown at the bottom of the opposite page, made of wood, steel, plastic and silver. If you do not have something silver, use another metal, such as a piece of copper pipe, or aluminium foil screwed into a long thin shape. You also need some dried beans (or peas), butter, hot water and a mug.

Put the things to be tested in the mug. Then use a tiny smear of butter to stick a bean on each thing.* Make sure all the beans are at the same height.

2

Fill the mug with boiling water and watch what happens. Note which objects lose their beans first.

Heat from the water travels up the objects and melts the butter so the beans fall off. The objects which lose their beans first are the ones through which heat travels fastest. These things are said to be good conductors of heat. You should find that the beans fall off the metal things first, showing that metals are good conductors of heat. There is another test over the page.

The experiment will not work if you use too much butter.

Battery test

Here is a test to show that metals conduct electricity. You need a 4.5 volt battery, a 3.5 volt bulb, a miniature bulb holder,* three pieces of fuse wire 20cm long, and a very small screwdriver. You also need the objects you tested on the previous page.

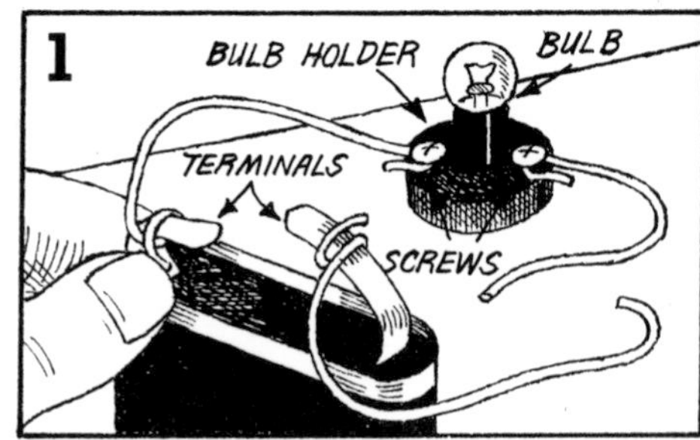

Attach a piece of wire to each of the battery terminals. Then wind one of the wires round one of the screws on the bulb holder. Put the third piece of wire round the other screw on the bulb holder.

If you hold the ends of the two loose wires together, the bulb should light. This shows there is an electric current flowing along the wires and through the bulb.

3

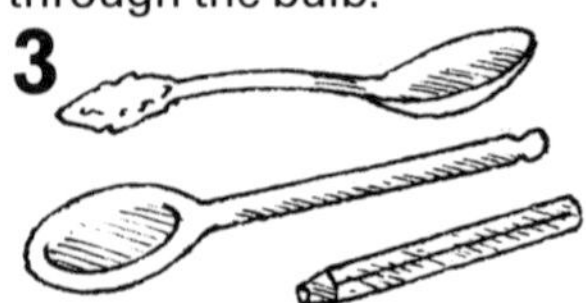

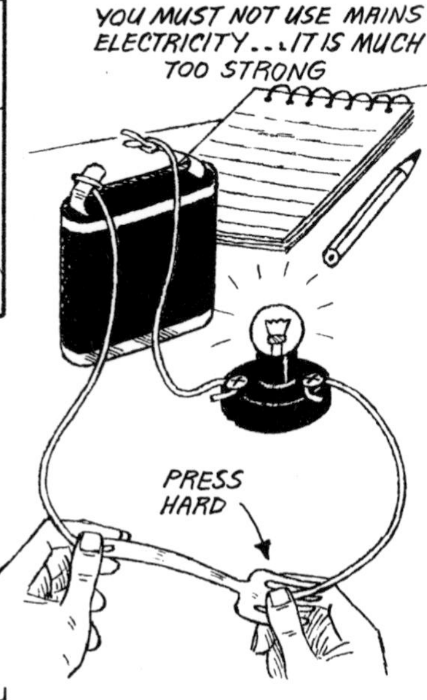

Now hold one of the objects you want to test between the two loose wires. Press the wires firmly on the object. If the electric current can flow through the substance of which the object is made, the bulb will light up.

Test all the objects and note which of them conduct electricity. Then compare your results with those of the heat test. You should find that all the metal objects conduct electricity and heat.

You can get these in electrical or hardware stores.

More things to test

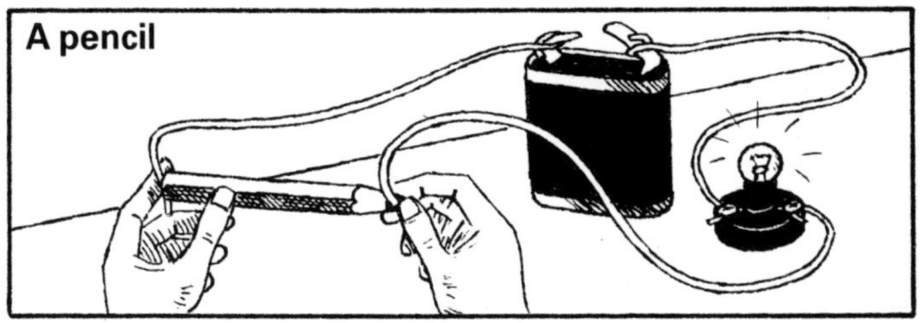

Try testing the lead in a pencil to see if it conducts electricity. Press one of the wires round the lead point of the pencil and the other against the lead on the flat end. The bulb should light up.

Pencil leads are made from an element called carbon. Carbon is an unusual element. It conducts electricity, but it does not have the other properties of metals, and it is not a metal.

Salty water

Dissolve four teaspoons of salt in half a jar of warm water. Then dip the two wires into the salty water and see what happens.

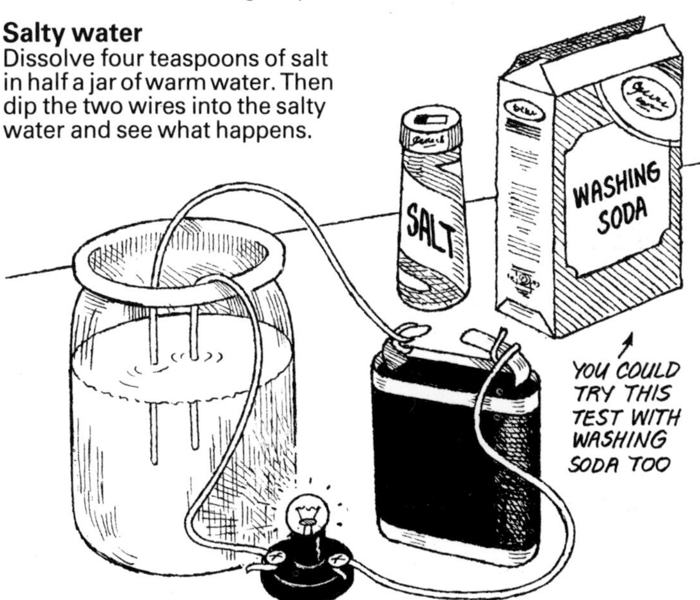

The bulb should glow faintly for a few seconds. This shows that the electric current from the two wires can flow through the salty water. The chemical name for salt is sodium chloride, and sodium is a metal. Anything that has a metal element in it conducts electricity when it is dissolved in water.

Copperplating a key

In this experiment you can cover an old key, or other metal object, with copper. You need a chemical called copper sulphate, which you can buy at some chemists and toyshops.* Take great care with it, as it is poisonous. You also need a 4.5 volt battery, some thin copper electric wire, scissors, sticky tape, glasspaper and a teaspoon. You must *not* use a kitchen teaspoon, as copper sulphate is poisonous.

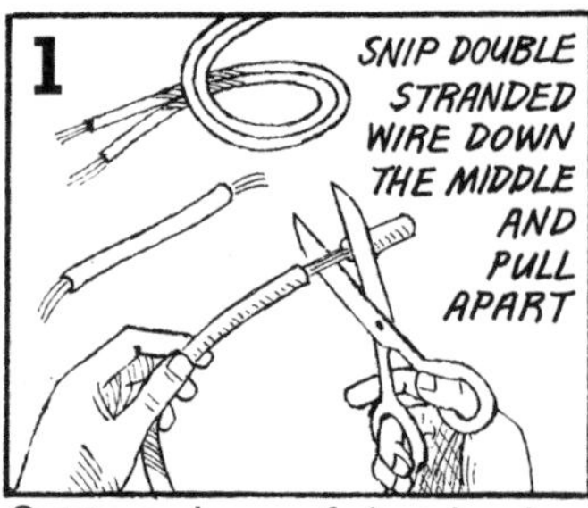

Cut two pieces of electric wire about 30cm long. Then, with scissors, strip off 3cm of the plastic at both ends of each wire.

Rub the key with glasspaper, then attach it to one of the wires.

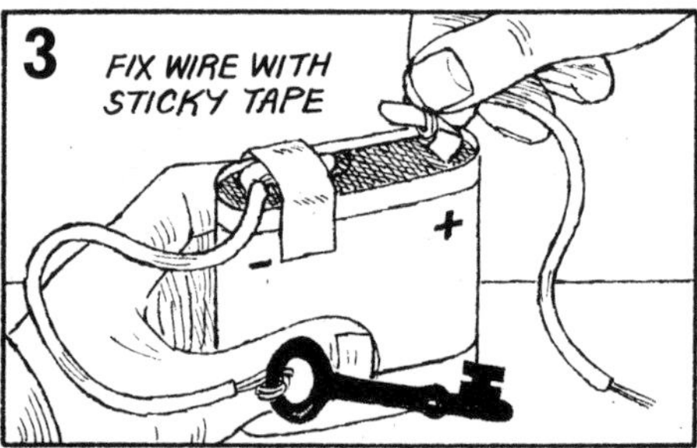

Look on the battery for the negative terminal (marked "–") and attach the wire with the key to it. Then attach the other wire to the positive terminal (marked "+").

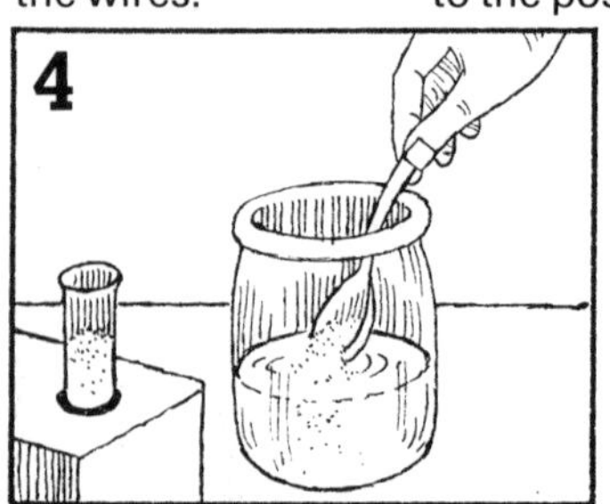

Fill the jar one third full with water and stir in two teaspoons of copper sulphate. Remember, you must not use a kitchen teaspoon.

Dip the key and the other wire into the copper sulphate solution and leave it for about 20 minutes. Make sure the key does not touch the other wire.

 You can find out more about buying chemicals from toyshops on page 60.

What happens

After about 20 minutes pull the key out and shake off any drops of copper sulphate into the jar. You should find the key has a pink coating of copper. This will turn orange if you leave it out in the air. You can find out how the copper is made below. If the key is not very well coated, put it back in the solution for a while.

If it does not work

Check that the wires are firmly attached to the battery terminals and that the wire from the key is attached to the negative terminal. If it still does not work, the battery may be flat. Test it in a torch, or just try the experiment again with a new battery.

How the copper is made

When copper sulphate dissolves in water it splits into copper parts and sulphate parts. When you dip the key and the wire into the solution, an electric current flows through it and the copper parts are attracted to the negative battery terminal. They move towards the negative terminal and collect around the key. Some of the copper also comes from the wire attached to the positive terminal. This wire is eaten away by the current and the copper goes into the solution.

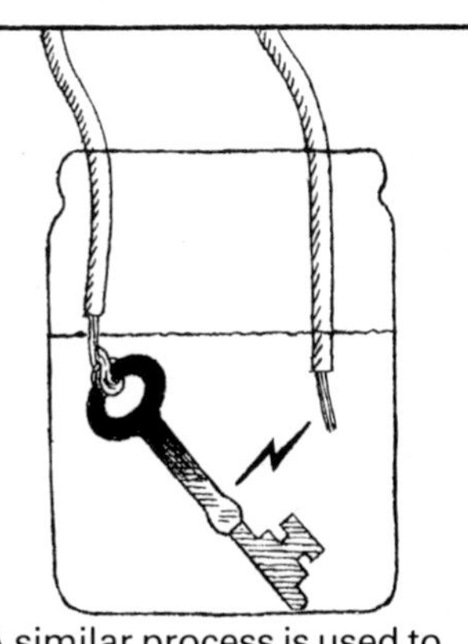

A similar process is used to put a thin coating of silver on jewellery and cutlery. This is called electroplating.

Equipment to make

Here are some ideas for chemistry equipment you can make yourself. Below there is a test-tube rack for holding test-tubes. Opposite you can find out how to measure out drops of liquid with a drinking straw, and how to make a measuring jug.

Over the page there is another way to make gas-catching equipment and instructions for how to make limewater.

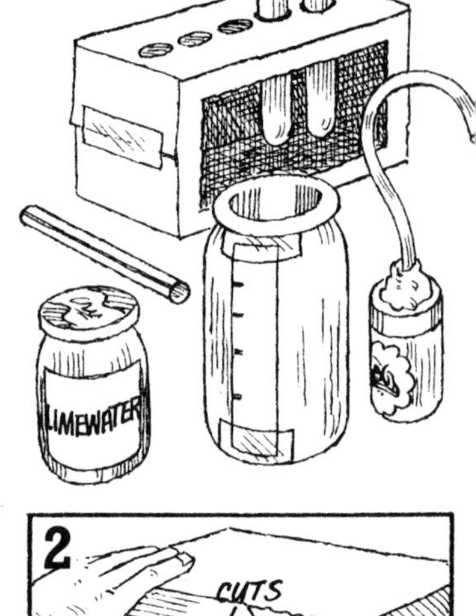

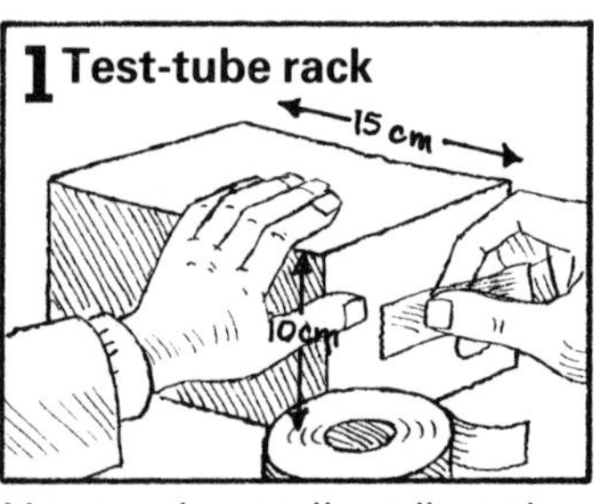

You need a small cardboard box about 10cm high and 15cm long. If the box opens at the ends, tape up the openings.

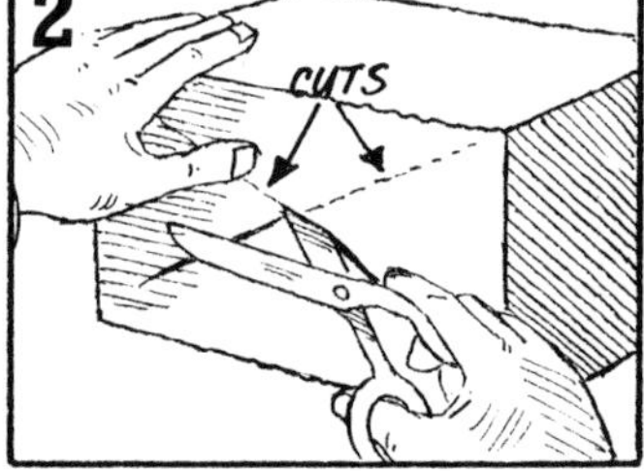

To cut out the front of the box, push the point of some scissors into the cardboard and make diagonal cuts to the corners. Do not cut right into the corners.

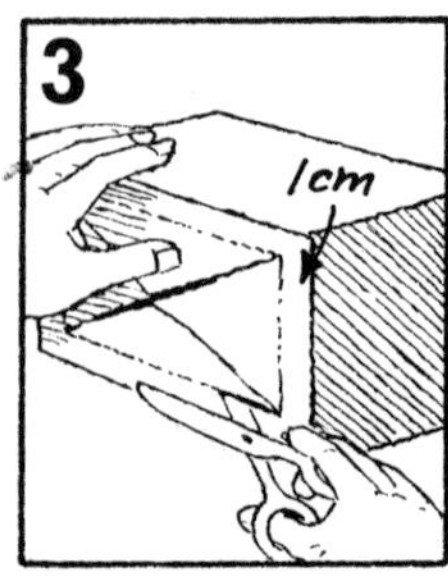

Then cut out the front of the box, leaving about 1cm round the edge.

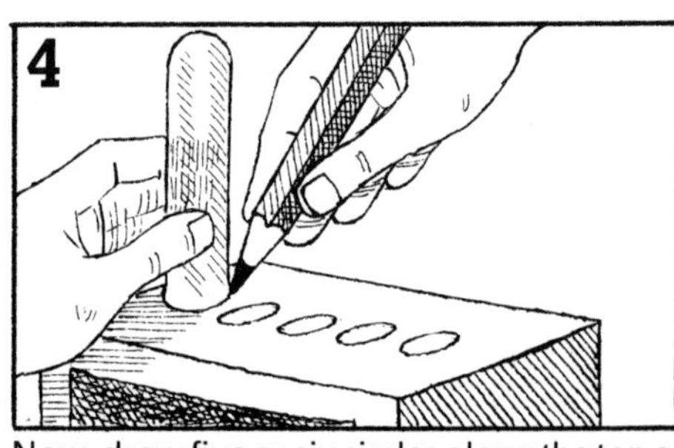

Now, draw five or six circles along the top of the box, by drawing round the top of a test-tube. Cut out the circles to make the holes for the test-tubes.

Drinking straw dropper

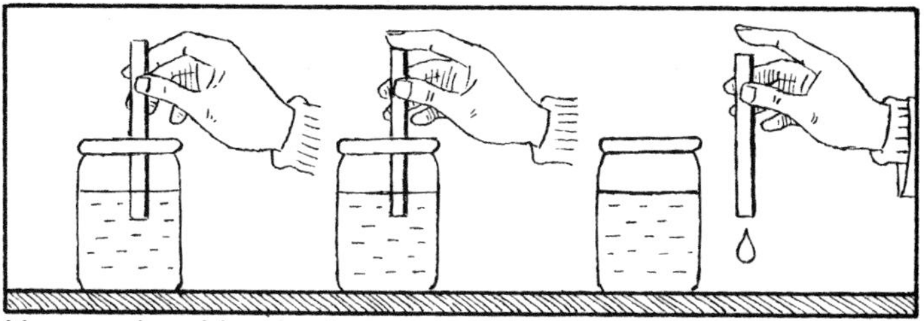

You need a wide, plastic straw. Cut a piece about 12cm long and dip it in some water. Then put your finger over the top and lift the straw out of the water. Some water is trapped inside.

To let one drop fall, lift your finger and replace it as soon as you see a drop forming on the end of the straw. You will need to practise until you can let just one drop fall at a time.

Measuring jar for chemicals

To make this you need a large, straight-sided jar and a measuring jug.

Stick a strip of paper down the side of the jar. Then, with the measuring jug, pour 125ml of water into the jar. Mark the level on the strip of paper.

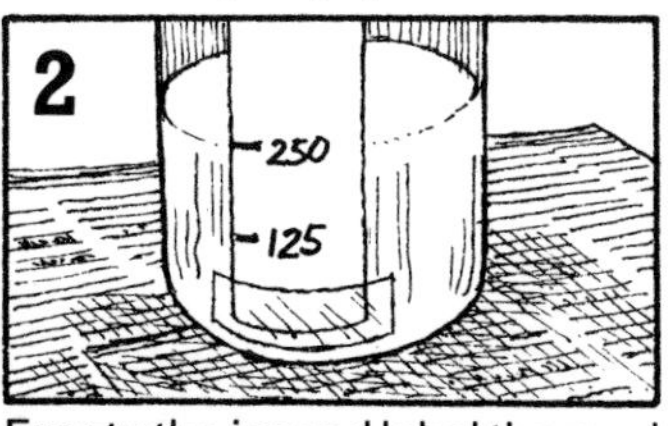

Empty the jar and label the mark 125ml. Then measure in 250ml and mark the water level again. Continue until you have all the measurements you want.

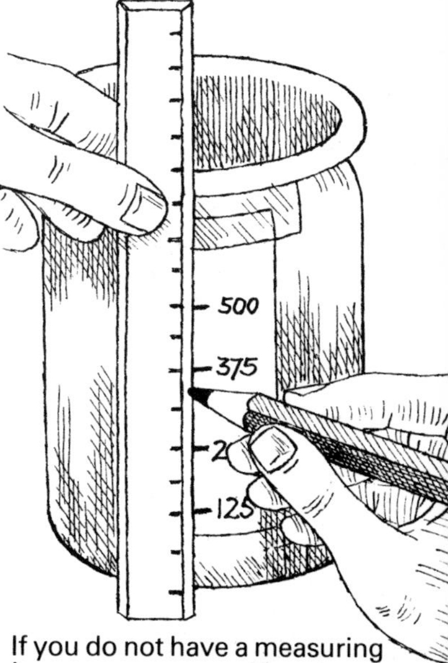

If you do not have a measuring jug, you can use a milk carton to pour 500ml of water into the jar.* Mark the level of the water, then empty the jar. Divide the distance below the mark into quarters.

**A milk carton holds 568ml so do not fill it right to the top.*

More gas-catching equipment

Here is a way to make gas-catching equipment for the gas tests if you do not have a test-tube. (If you have a test-tube you can make the equipment as shown on page 31.)

To make the equipment shown here you need some plasticine, a piece of plastic tubing about 40cm long, a blunt knife and a small container with a soft plastic lid (such as a pill box or a bubblebath container). It is best if the container is see-through, so you can see what is happening inside.

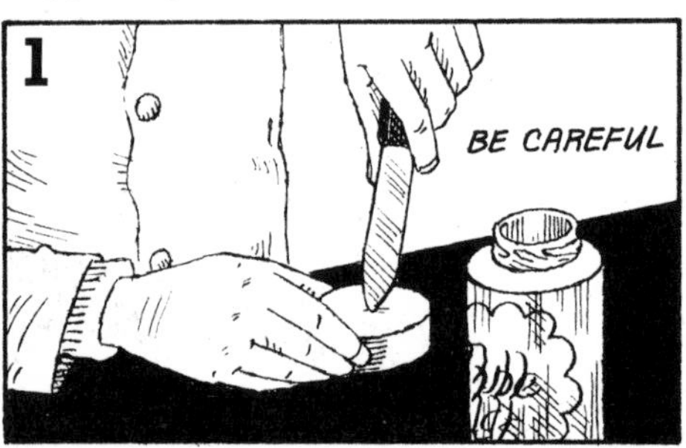

Push the point of the knife into the lid of the container, as shown above. Twist the knife round to make a hole just big enough for the plastic tubing to fit through.

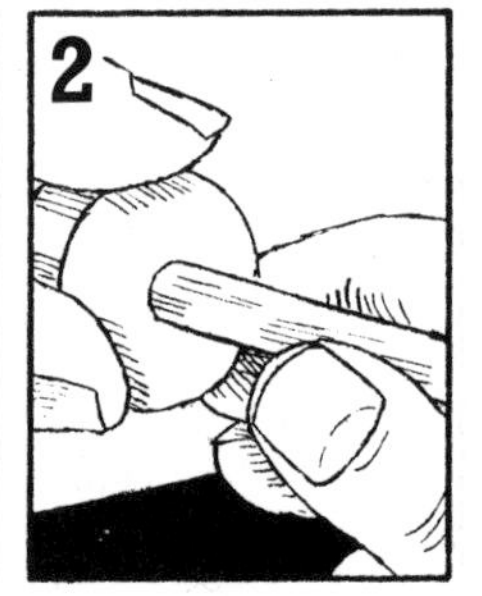

Then push one end of the plastic tubing into the hole in the lid.

On the top of the lid press plasticine round the tube to seal any gaps.

Make a gas in the container as shown in the experiment you are doing. Then catch the gas by screwing the cap on as fast as you can.

Making limewater

You may be able to buy limewater from a chemist, but if not, it is quite easy to make your own. You need a chemical called calcium hydroxide, which is also known as slaked lime.

Where to get slaked lime

Test-tubes of slaked lime are sold as refills for chemistry sets, so you may be able to buy some from a toyshop (see page 60).

You can also buy slaked lime from a gardening shop. It is sold as "garden lime". Before you buy garden lime, though, check on the packet that it is made from calcium hydroxide or hydrated lime. Do not buy garden lime made from calcium carbonate or calcium oxide.

1 How to make it

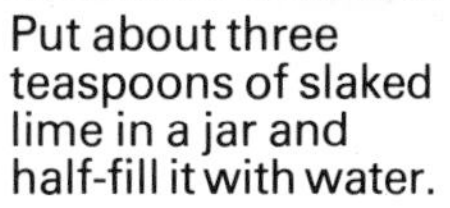
Put about three teaspoons of slaked lime in a jar and half-fill it with water.

2

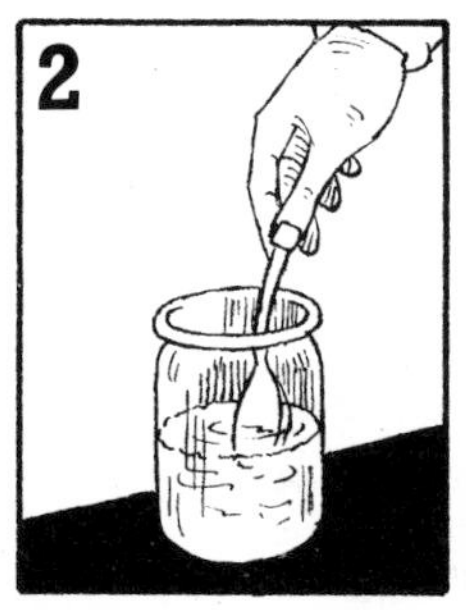

Stir and leave it to settle for about four hours until the liquid clears.

3

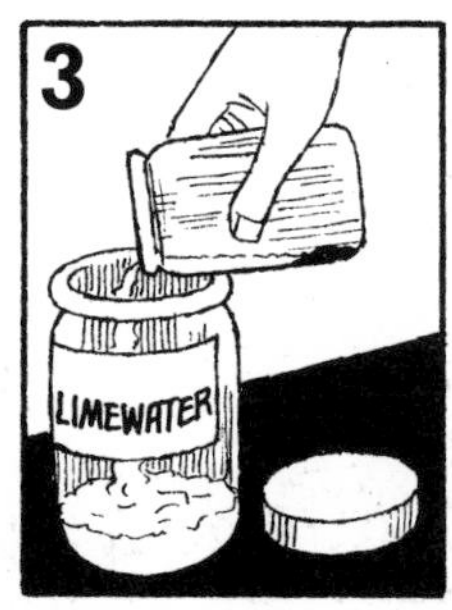

Pour the clear limewater into a labelled jar and put the lid on.

4

You can make more limewater by adding water to the lime left in the bottom of the jar, stirring and leaving it to settle as before.

Limewater check

If the limewater experiments do not work, it may be because the lime you used was not calcium hydroxide. You can check your limewater by blowing into it through a straw for a minute or two.* It should turn cloudy. If it does not, it is not proper limewater. You need to buy some more slaked lime. Make sure it is calcium hydroxide.

**Take care not to suck any of the liquid into your mouth.*

Buying chemicals

Most of the chemicals you need are household substances which you can buy from supermarkets. Below, there is a chart giving the chemical names of some common substances. Then there is a list showing where you can buy some of the more unusual ones. At the bottom of the page you can find out how to buy chemicals in chemists and toyshops.

Chemical names

Vinegar	Ethanoic acid
Lemon juice	Citric acid
Tea	Tannic acid
Sour milk	Lactic acid
Washing soda	Sodium carbonate
Bicarbonate of soda	Sodium hydrogen carbonate
Salt	Sodium chloride
Slaked lime	Calcium hydroxide

Where to buy chemicals

Citric acid crystals – Winemaking store

Washing soda – Hardware store

Bicarbonate of soda – Supermarket

Cream of tartar – Supermarket

Slaked lime – Toyshop, gardening shop

Copper sulphate* – Toyshop, chemist

Phenolphthalein – Chemist (ask for laxative pills and check they contain this chemical).

Distilled water – Garage, chemist (you may have to take your own container).

Iodine – Chemist (ask for red tincture of iodine).

Chemists

When you go to a chemist ask at the dispensary counter for the chemical you want and tell the assistant what it is for. Always take great care with chemicals, as they may be poisonous. Use them only in the way suggested in this book and wash them away as soon as you have finished.

Toyshops

Toyshops sell small test-tubes of chemicals as refills for chemistry sets. If your toyshop does not stock these, you can write to a chemistry set manufacturer and ask them to send you the refills. To find the address, look on the box of a chemistry set, or ask in a toyshop.

*Copper sulphate is poisonous, so keep it in a jar marked "harmful"

Where to buy equipment

Eyedropper – You can buy one of these very cheaply from a chemist.

Plastic tubing – Also called syphon tubing. You can buy it at winemaking stores.

Plastic funnel – These are sold in hardware stores.

Batteries – You can buy batteries in electrical stores and many other kinds of stores.

Fuse wire and copper electric wire – These are sold in electrical and hardware stores.

Miniature bulb holder and bulb – Electrical and hardware stores sell these.

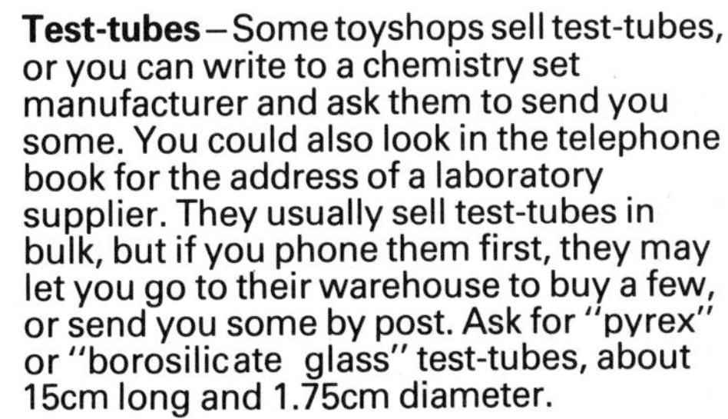

Test-tubes – Some toyshops sell test-tubes, or you can write to a chemistry set manufacturer and ask them to send you some. You could also look in the telephone book for the address of a laboratory supplier. They usually sell test-tubes in bulk, but if you phone them first, they may let you go to their warehouse to buy a few, or send you some by post. Ask for "pyrex" or "borosilicate glass" test-tubes, about 15cm long and 1.75cm diameter.

Answer to chemical muddle puzzle (page 38)

This chart shows how each powder should react in the tests. Match your results with the chart in order to identify your five powders.

	Cream of tartar	Salt	Bicarbonate of soda	Flour	Sugar
Indicator test	Acid	Alkali	Alkali	Neutral	Neutral
Water test	Dissolved	Dissolved	Dissolved	Did not dissolve	Dissolved
Gas test	No gas	No gas	Carbon dioxide gas	No gas	No gas

Equipment lists

These two pages list all the things you need for the experiments. The experiments are grouped together by subject and all the equipment for each group of experiments is listed together. The numbers in brackets show the pages on which the experiments appear.

Acid tests (10-15)
Knife
Wooden spoon
Teaspoon
Saucepan
Funnel
Paper towels
Bottle with a top
About 10 jars
Eyedropper*
Labels
Scissors
Pen
Notepad
Boiling water
Red cabbage (or rose petals or blackberries)
For testing:
Lemon juice
Orange juice
Tea
Bicarbonate of soda
Baking powder
Vinegar
Cola drink
Boiled sweet
Washing-up liquid
Washing soda
Liquid floor cleaner
Sour milk
Indigestion tablets
Milk of magnesia

Water tests (16-19)
Distilled water
Tap water
Boiled water
Six jars
Teaspoon
Tablespoon
Grater (or knife)
Bar of soap
Washing soda
Eyedropper
Labels
Scissors
Notepad
Felt-tip pen

How to make bath salts (20-21)
Washing soda
Cologne or perfume
Food colouring
Tablespoon
Rolling pin
Bowl
Polythene bag
Jar with lid
Saucer
Labels
Scissors
Pen

Soap tests (22-23)
Three or four makes of washing powder
Butter or margarine
Warm water
Five jars
Teaspoon
Knife
Kitchen scales
Scissors
Rag
Labels
Pen
Notepad
Red cabbage indicator*

Soap powder eats egg experiment (24-25)
Biological soap powder
Ordinary soap powder
Egg (hardboiled)
Tablespoon or measuring jar
Teaspoon
Knife
Scissors
Two jars
Labels
Pen

Food tests (26-29)
Tincture of iodine
Jar
Test-tube (or jar)
Large mug
Saucer or jar lid
Teaspoon
Tablespoon
Eyedropper
Cold water
Boiling water
Flour
Newspaper
Clock or watch

Things to test:
Apple
Potato
Salt
Butter
Rice
Cheese
Meat
White paper
Paper glue
Laundry starch

Making gas (31-35)
Three or four jars
Test-tube
Plastic tubing
Plasticine
Ruler
Scissors
Teaspoon
Drinking straw
Labels
Pen
Washing soda
Limewater (see page 31)
Vinegar

Some or all of the following:
A lemon
A grapefruit
Cola drink
Sour milk
continued above ▶

This is useful, but not essential.

and some or all of these:
Bicarbonate of soda
Limestone or chalk from the ground (not blackboard chalk)
An eggshell

Making fizzy drinks (36-37)

Bicarbonate of soda
Citric acid crystals
Icing sugar
A still drink
A bottle of fizzy drink
Kitchen teaspoon
Kitchen tablespoon
Bowl
Two jars with lids
Labels
Scissors
Pen
Gas-catching equipment (see page 31)
Limewater (see page 31)

Chemical muddle puzzle (38-39)

Flour
Salt
Icing sugar
Bicarbonate of soda
Cream of tartar
Vinegar or other acid
Warm water
Teaspoon
Five jars
Five test-tubes (or five more jars)
Labels
Scissors
Pen
Notepad
Gas-catching equipment (see page 31)
Limewater (see page 31)
Red cabbage indicator (see page 10)

Testing inks and dyes (40-42)

Four or five dark-coloured felt-tip pens
Two different black felt-tip pens
Blotting paper
Ruler
Scissors
Saucer
Jar
Water
Sugar-coated sweets (e.g. "Smarties")

Invisible inks (43-45)

Paper
Paintbrush
Biro

For lemon juice ink:
Eggcup or small jar
Lemon
Clock or watch

For phenolphthalein ink:
Laxative pills containing phenolphthalein
Washing soda
Hot water
Two jars
Two teaspoons
Blunt knife
Tablespoon
Plate
Ruler

How to split water (46-47)

Two pencils
Pencil sharpener
Ruler
Scissors
Paper
Sticky tape
A thick book
Jar
Water
9 volt battery
15 amp fuse wire

Sorting out elements (50-53)

Long thin objects made from wood, plastic, steel, silver (or another metal, e.g. copper)
Notepad
Pen

For the heat test:
Dried beans or peas
Butter or margarine
Boiling water
Mug

For the battery test:
4.5 volt battery
15 amp fuse wire
3.5 volt bulb
Miniature bulb holder
Small screwdriver
Ruler
Scissors
Sticky tape
Pencil
Teaspoon
Jar
Water
Salt

Copperplating a key (54-55)

Old key or other metal object
Copper sulphate
Glasspaper
4.5 volt battery
Thin copper electric wire
Scissors
Ruler
Sticky tape
Teaspoon (not a kitchen one)
Jar
Water
Clock or watch

ERC idea book c1974

Index